Karine Lambert is a photographer and novelist. Her first novel, *L'Immeuble des femmes qui ont renoncé aux hommes*, sold more than 120,000 copies in France. *Now Let's Dance* has sold in nine territories, and is already a bestseller in France and Germany.

NOW LET'S DANCE

KARINE LAMBERT

*Translated from the French
by Anthea Bell*

WEIDENFELD & NICOLSON

First published in Great Britain in 2017
by Weidenfeld & Nicolson
an imprint of the Orion Publishing Group Ltd
Carmelite House, 50 Victoria Embankment
London EC4Y 0DZ

An Hachette UK Company

1 3 5 7 9 10 8 6 4 2

First published in French as *Eh Bien Dansons Maintenant!*
by Editions Jean-Claude Lattès in 2016

A CIP catalogue record for this book is
available from the British Library.

ISBN (Hardback) 978 1 4746 0529 8
ISBN (Export Trade Paperback) 978 1 4746 0530 4
ISBN (eBook) 978 1 4746 0532 8

Typeset at The Spartan Press Ltd,
Lymington, Hants

Printed and bound in Great Britain by Clays Ltd,
St Ives plc

www.orionbooks.co.uk

To the first love
And the last love

It's time to set the stars alight again

Guillaume Apollinaire

1

In the end she had chosen the mahogany one with four copper handles. Model 328: twenty-two millimetres thick, satin lining, insect-proof, waterproof. 'Built to last,' according to the undertaker's assistant. Proof against everything. Except eternal rest.

'It's up to you, madame.'

For the last three days that phrase had been echoing through her mind like a hammer blow. It was up to her to decide whether the coffin was to be open or closed, if the photograph was to be in colour or black and white, if the caterer was to provide sandwiches or rolls with assorted fillings. And was it absolutely necessary to deck the funeral wreath with a white ribbon saying, *To my dear husband?*

'It's up to you, madame.'

. . .

Slim in her pearl-grey suit, a discreet lipstick matching the blusher on her cheeks, she stares at the grave. Dignified and impeccably dressed, the way Henri liked her. Fifty-five years and seventeen days of marriage. The only man she had ever slept with, the only man who had seen her naked. Twenty thousand and ninety-two shared awakenings, and then one last morning. Lying in his twin bed, he hadn't opened his eyes. The death notice said, *Died quietly in his sleep.* A deviation from the normal etiquette that his only son, Frédéric, had not appreciated.

Impossible to think of him there, inside the box that the gravediggers are going to lower into the hole in the ground before covering with earth. Familiar figures surround her: Dr Dubois, the local bigwigs, distant cousins from the countryside. Her faithful Maria gives her a discreet little nod. From now on Marguerite Delorme will be known as the notary's widow. Beside her, in a black suit, Frédéric is holding her elbow while biting his lower lip to repress any show of emotion. Carole, her daughter-in-law, has her hand on their son Ludovic's shoulder. In church just now, he paid a brief tribute to his grandfather, with whom he shared few words but the same passion for tennis. The little boy was trembling as he read from his piece of paper; then he had come back to sit beside his grandmother, who had patted his cheek. Moved, Carole had looked away.

. . .

The undertaker's men are letting the coffin down into the hole. She closes her eyes and squeezes Ludovic's hand. Her son is holding her elbow even more firmly. When the ropes are pulled away, she feels that the worst is behind her.

People file past: Madame Thingummy's little bow, Monsieur So-and-So's comment; how is she supposed to react? She courteously accepts the storm of condolences.

'Eighty-five is a good age.'

'He led an exemplary life.'

'Be brave.'

Strangers take her hand and hold it for a long time, in silence. Who will come next? She wonders whether someone will become confused and offer her their heartfelt congratulations instead.

Then it will be time for the waltz of finger food and coffee cups. Yesterday she had visualised how the ceremony would progress, and now here it is – the real thing. Her thoughts are muddled by a sleepless night and the unusual September warmth.

She tells each person, 'I'll be fine.'

As if she were the one who had to comfort them. And because she has nothing left to hope for now. She doesn't believe in the great reunion in a world beyond the grave. They were Henri and Maggy. Now there's only Maggy.

. . .

She declined to have the reception in the hall next to the church. She prefers the comfort of her own home, surrounded by her own furniture and ornaments. A point of reference in the middle of a situation that she can't control any more. The way other people look at her redefines her: she has shifted into sepia. Muffled voices mingle in her head: 'You really ought to have a good cry'; 'Do sit down'; 'Have something to drink'; 'Would you like a cup of tea, an aspirin, a tranquilliser?'

She repeats the only words still at her command. 'I'll be fine.'

On the doorstep, Frédéric kisses her on the forehead, as he has always seen his father kiss her. Ludovic nestles close to her skirt and murmurs, 'I love you, Granny.'

Suddenly her sitting room seems huge. Yes, she will be fine. She will round the Cape of Good Hope, cross the Atlantic, and then, if she has any strength left, she will climb Everest. Henri would certainly have thought she hadn't laid on enough goat-cheese petits fours.

She sways, reaches out to the small, round table to keep her balance and the vase of carnations falls over. She looks at the broken glass, the water soaking into the carpet, and the dying flowers bring tears to her eyes. He was always the one who locked the front door, in fact double-locked it. 'You can never be too careful,' he used to say. She takes off her shoes, the jacket of her grey widow's suit, and drops onto the divan, feeling helpless. She misses Hélène. Her sister would have put her arms around her, gathering in her grief. What would she have thought of the three Chopin sonatas played during the service? 'You should have played a nice bit of rock to get those good folk moving.' Her darling Hélène is never far away.

Automatically she switches on the TV, which keeps up its eternal transmission of the same games, with the same laughter and shrieks from the winners. 'Pathetic and ridiculous,' her husband would have said. She looks at the empty armchair where he always sat. With a Scotch on the table beside him, he would switch from a political debate to a programme on economics, while she buried herself in a book. Without a glance, without words of love, but with neither voice ever rising higher than the other. A man and a woman, two bodies and two minds. He: straight and stiff as a notarial deed. She: a candle flame trembling but not yet extinguished. Having inherited the remote control, she doesn't know which keys to press. On screen, there is a Japanese documentary about tuna fishing.

When Henri came home from the office, he would open the front door of the house silently, hang up his hat and coat in the hall and, without letting her know that he was back, disappear into his study, emerging only when she announced, 'Dinner is ready.'

On the first day of their life together, he had issued his orders. As a name, Marguerite was too long, too flowery, and Maggy was a better match with Henri. Her baptismal name was no longer spoken, except on rare occasions, and never within her husband's hearing. She was not to have a job outside the home. His sole concession was her voluntary work at the municipal library twice a week. She was always to wear dresses and arrange her hair in a chignon, as she had when they first met. They would not have any pets. Only one child, preferably a boy. And in a tone that brooked no contradiction he concluded, 'It would be desirable for us to continue using the formal *vous* to each other.'

Luckily Frédéric had come along. When their son was born, Henri had landed the boy with his favourite composer's first name and, shortly before he was six years old, had enrolled him at the Saint-Roch boarding school. Marguerite had wept, but she comforted herself by thinking that her only child would be happier surrounded by companions of his own age. She looked forward to seeing him at the weekends, when she organised picnics and outings to the pony club to make his Saturdays and Sundays memorable. The other days of the week were spent with Henri. He bought *Le Monde* every morning, and commented on the fluctuations in the stock market at dinner, in between the soup and the dessert. Marguerite listened politely to this gibberish, nodding from time to time. And on the first Thursday of every month, Maria polished the silver. Henri and Maggy Delorme were entertaining their friends.

At the beginning of their marriage, Henri used to take baths full to the brim with bubbles. He could stay in there for half an hour, his eyes closed, his torso emerging from the water, humming a few notes in a musical voice that was almost pleasing, and was never heard at any other time. A few metres away from the half-open bathroom door, Maggy used to wait for him to call out and invite her to join him. One day she ventured to say, 'I do like it when you sing in the bath.' He had locked the door. She put her ear close to it, so that she could still hear him, listening for the eddies of sound.

They were a civilised couple; there were no surprises and no arguments between them. The only sign language that he allowed himself was a raised eyebrow or an expression of disapproval. She, patient and discreet, never betraying her innermost thoughts, had adjusted to his personality. She had never been with another man, and in the absence of maternal advice on how to be with her husband, their time together rolled by without any instructions. Their nights were as dignified and blameless as their days. However, Maggy was sure that this upright and modest man loved her in his fashion.

Motionless, wearing a flannel dressing gown and velour slippers, in front of a Japanese fisherman brandishing a tuna on the end of his harpoon, Marguerite murmurs, 'I'm seventy-eight years old. What am I going to do with my life?'

2

Marcel Guedj comes out of the cinema and casts a last glance at the poster for the film *El Gusto*. He doesn't want to go down the steps to the Métro, still less to go home. Hands in his pockets, he strolls along the Grands Boulevards. He hadn't set foot in a cinema for months, and the men in the film, separated for fifty years and then reunited to play Chaâbi music and relive their youth, have overwhelmed him. So he goes on walking along the streets of Paris at random, looking back to the day in November 1954 when he left his country.

His father had felt the change coming. The separatists had plundered their farm and nothing would ever be the same again. They had to leave before the situation grew worse and the sky went completely dark. The family left behind their home near the river and the tombs of their ancestors. Marcel had to abandon his teacher, his classmates and the football pitch. He had just been promoted to centre-forward, and was to have played in his new position the following week. They gave their dog, Oscar, to a neighbour. She promised to look after him, and swore he'd still be there when they came back. No one really thought they would, but they all pretended to believe in the impossible.

A first cousin who lived in the capital had sent a letter that Marcel's father proudly read aloud to his sons:

Dear André,

We are looking forward to seeing you — you, your wife and little Marcel, who must be quite big by now. I've found you an apartment not far from your future job. Because yes, believe it or not, I've found you a position as a gardener with the local authority in Vincennes, so you'll still be close to the earth that you love so much. The apartment will be a tight squeeze, but as you often say, one day the wind will blow in the right direction again. And I have more good news: I've found a furnished apartment for your friends and their daughter, Nora, if they're still coming with you.

When I came back to France ten years ago and I saw the words 'Liberty-Equality-Fraternity' carved in large letters on the pediment of a town hall, I said to myself, You can stop searching now; this is the place.

Olga is looking forward to seeing you too. Call me when you get to Marseille and tell me which train you'll be catching. It will come in to the Gare de Lyon, and I'll be there to meet you. Have a good crossing.

Affectionately,

Your cousin Maurice

Robert, the elder son, who was nineteen at that point and a mechanic, still believed in French Algeria and had decided to stay on, come what may. Marcel had refused to hug him goodbye, preferring to leave without looking back. Two brothers tossed around by circumstances they could not control.

The family had packed in haste, taking the tea set and the pressure cooker, leaving the mattresses. They left their house by night, leaving their washing out on the balcony so that it would look as if someone was still there. Their furniture would follow later. As for the rest, *inshallah!*

Their neighbours, the Ben Soussans and their daughter, Nora, were also on the move. They faced the same choice between escaping the violence or trusting in a situation that had become disturbing. The prospect of their company went some way to soothing Marcel's bruised heart: Nora would be coming as well. He used to take her up to the hilltops, where they would exchange vows as light as air, and he would show her the sinuous pathways across the sky between the Great Bear and the Coma Berenices. A childhood blessed by the gods.

There was nothing to suggest an exodus on dock number 3. Tourists were disembarking; the orange seller hadn't shut up shop; life went on as if all the assassinations at the beginning of the month had never taken place. Only several disembowelled houses foreshadowed what was still to come. Anyway, André had made his decision and he was sticking to it. The front page of *L'Écho d'Alger* had said, 'Make sure you leave in good time.' Marcel considered his father a hero. He had absolute confidence in him, and would have followed him to the ends of the earth, no questions asked.

At six thirty in the evening on 29 November 1954, the *Sidi Mabrouk* left the port of Algiers. The crossing to Marseille would take twelve hours. Handkerchiefs were waved: tiny farewells as lives were split in two. Passengers with haggard faces clung to the ship's rail, aware that they would not return to this land where five generations had lived before them. Dazed, and with a sinking heart, they watched the mountains disappear behind the white houses of el-Bahdja, 'the Radiant', and their country slipped away. Despair at leaving everything and fear of the unknown showed in their eyes. For the first time the boy saw his father shed tears. Grown men become children once more when they leave their native land.

Marcel was looking up at the Milky Way. No sky could ever measure up to that one. At the age of twelve, he firmly believed that these stars were unique to his country and he would never see them again. Although just now, only one thing mattered to him: Nora's hand in his. Two children crossing a vast sea to a country about which they knew nothing. They had been told, 'We're going to Vincennes, near Paris, the capital of France. We'll see the Eiffel Tower, a huge construction made of iron matchsticks.'

Marcel's parents had finally gone to sleep next to their three cardboard suitcases and two jute bags. Far off, on the other side of the deck, someone struck up a popular old song. An accordion, a banjo, a tambourine, like black horses galloping along, then the slow, sad quavering of a flute, rising like a soul lost in the mist, mingling with male and female voices. The Chaâbi music tugged at their heartstrings, as it had at the village festivals. Jews, Muslims, Christians, French and Algerians, all united. Marcel had closed his eyes. Lulled by the melody, he was no longer afraid, and he had promised himself that life would be good in the little town of Vincennes, since Nora was going to be there too.

. . .

He moves away from the Grands Boulevards. Walking does him good. He wants to zoom in and out of the scenes from his past.

Pressing close together, surrounded by their belongings, like a clan of emigrants, the Guedj and Ben Soussan families formed a motley group outside the Gare de Lyon. Walls of a dirty grey colour as far as the eye could see, narrow façades, an anaemic geranium forgotten on a windowsill, a uniform sky, a fine drizzle. So this was the capital of France?

They moved into the temporary apartment in Vincennes found by Cousin Maurice. It was terribly cold that first winter, and there was only one solid-fuel stove, in the kitchen. They could boil a kettle to wash in the evenings, but had to use ice-cold water in the mornings. Marcel no longer belonged to Algeria, but he didn't belong in this city either. A concrete playground had replaced trodden earth, chestnut and orange trees, and rain hid the sun. Luckily he and Nora went to the same school. The two families met to share spiced meatballs, the mint-tea ritual – sitting quietly in a corner of the local park – and the therapeutic virtues of Chaâbi music. The two fathers would play and sing it to the end of their days. Marcel and Nora invented hills in the woods of Vincennes, and tried to tame their new universe by playing hide-and-seek in the local alleyways. They no longer rode a donkey or caught salamanders in the rocks; they discovered baguettes and sausage; they became inhabitants of the city.

He was about to celebrate his fifteenth birthday when the news broke. It was worse than a sandstorm. Nora hadn't been to school that day. When he got home, his father was waiting for him on the doorstep. He simply said, 'Nora's grandmother has been taken to hospital – it's an emergency. Her parents had no choice. They've all gone back to Algeria.'

After that, life, for Marcel, became a succession of arrivals and departures. Without Nora, Vincennes held no interest for Marcel, and he missed Algeria more than ever. During sleepless nights the same question went round and round in his head: why didn't she come to say goodbye to me? Her silence gnawed at his heart. And as for him, why had he never dared kiss her?

But once more daily life took over. There was a big box under the Christmas tree with a telescope in it, and every evening as he watched the stars in the sky above Vincennes, he told himself that back in Algeria she might be watching them too.

His parents enrolled him at a vocational secondary school, where he did his baccalaureate. All his classmates had already chosen a trade, while he lost himself in impossible dreams and came up against the awkward four corners of life. He worked in a garage for a month, to feel closer to his brother, but he hated the smell of grease. 'What are we going to do with you?' his father had said. During the school holidays he had taken a little job at Vincennes Zoo. The exiled animals fascinated him, and so he applied for the post of zookeeper, which was about to fall vacant. Co-workers without any past or any imagination gave way to more unusual colleagues. He came to know every scale on the python in enclosure number 37, which he passed each morning; the turtle with a bandaged foot; the Bengal tiger whose whiskers moved upwards as if it were laughing. And he plunged, amazed, into this jungle in the middle of the city, with its smell of sawdust and mouse droppings, searching for that rare bird that no one else had ever seen. He felt at home in this little paradise.

He had spent seven years alongside the gentle elegance of the giraffes and the mischief of the monkeys. Then one day, hidden under postal orders and an advertisement for a large new superstore, a postcard arrived for him, postmarked Mouzaïa, Algeria. *I'm coming back. I miss Vincennes. And that's not the only thing I miss. Nora.*

3

'It's been a long time, Madame Delorme. I've got rump steak, or some nice veal escalopes. Would you like two, the same as usual? Two escalopes, thinly sliced?'

'I'll take just the one today, please.'

'Something different for your husband?'

It's so difficult to say the words: he's defunct, deceased, dead. She doesn't like these definitive terms, and the sympathetic expression they bring to other people's faces. Bereavement nails her to the ground, and she doesn't know how to confront it.

'No, thank you. He's away.'

Everyone in Maisons-Laffitte knew Maître Delorme the notary. The butcher will soon find out that she was lying, but for now she keeps banging up against the harsh corners of reality. She wishes she were transparent. Her distress is a private matter.

She searches in her wallet for the money that her son

has given her for day-to-day expenses, just as Henri used to. If she is thinking of buying something larger, she is to ask for his approval, because from now on he will be in charge of her finances. He has asked her to keep all her receipts. Suppose it came into her head to treat herself to a jasmine tea with a chocolate eclair?

'Don't forget your package. Have a nice day.'

'And the same to you.'

Like a plant that has lost its supporting stake, she must now learn how to manage on her own. Small steps to begin with. A plate, a knife, a fork and spoon, a glass, a napkin in its silver ring. And sitting alone in the large dining room. After a week she decided to eat in the kitchen instead. On Friday she replaced the usual fish with pasta shells and butter — something her husband didn't like — switched on the radio to break the silence, pecked at her food, then threw the rest away. She surprised herself by swearing several times.

Henri used to stack the dishwasher in silence, and according to a ritual that never changed. First the glasses, then their two plates, one behind the other, and only then the cutlery, all neatly aligned. He wouldn't let her wash their few dishes herself, because he said the detergent would spoil her hands. She took that as a sign of his love.

She strokes her hands gently, and thinks that she could

have worn rubber gloves. It's too late now. She looks at the sink as if her life has stopped right there.

How many hours must she shuck off before it is time for bed? He never wanted any shutters or even a curtain over the French window that leads into the garden. All those tall trees at the end cast alarming shadows. Suppose there is someone hiding there? Just suppose that someone taps on the window in the middle of the night? A stranger, his nose glued to the glass. With Henri, she never experienced that fear, but now it returns to her like the terror of a little girl. She remembers playing hide-and-seek with Hélène one day. After a quarter of an hour she still hadn't managed to find her, so she sat down on the ground in tears, sure that she had lost her for ever. The sorrows of childhood cling to our skin.

She had gone straight from her parents' house to her husband's. A tepid life, free from anxiety or any all-consuming passion.

What if a fuse blows?

What if she can't get the lid off the jam jar?

What if she slips in the bath?

However, she has absolutely no intention of moving, let alone of going to live with her son. Last weekend he said, 'Carole's aunt is in a retirement home, living with people of her own age. She's not so lonely now, and we don't have to worry.' What will they do with her? Leave her out on the pavement one day when the dustbin men are coming to collect the rubbish?

As if he could read her thoughts, her son added, 'Maman, it's for her own good.'

Since then she has shut herself away at home. She has taken the early novels of Françoise Sagan from her bookshelves and, page after page, she tries to forget – at least for a few moments – that letter from the bank. *From 1 October all information will be sent to you electronically. Please let us know your email address.* She feels lost in a world that is moving forward much faster than she can. Last week the cash machine swallowed her card. She tapped the keys frantically, to no avail. In the queue behind her, a woman had called out, 'Hey, old lady, you're wasting our time.' But who could she ask for help? Madame Leonard was no longer behind her window inside the bank. Marguerite had enjoyed hearing about Floriane, Madame Leonard's granddaughter, who is the same age as Ludovic.

She has no email address, only a fountain pen and some notepaper. She is afraid of the unexpected, afraid of dying, afraid of living alone. Afraid of being afraid. All through their childhood her big sister had always led the way. The intrepid Hélène had made her jump into the water, run until she was out of breath, pick blackberries and get their black juice all over her face. She had never needed any other friend. They swapped clothes, ate *pain au chocolat* together, shared all their secrets. Both of them on one or the other's bed, legs entwined, they read and reread *Sophie's Misfortunes* and *Little Women*, then amused themselves by acting out the adventures of their favourite characters. Hélène always took the boy's part and played Sophie's cousin, Paul, even though Marguerite was always a little too well behaved for the role of Sophie. They shared the same wild laughter many years later. Hélène adored fashion, and her younger sister would sometimes join her in Paris for one of the New Look fashion shows. In 1956 she had managed to get them tickets for the official launch of the bikini at the Piscine Molitor. And one afternoon they had been invited to the French premiere of *Rebel Without a Cause*, where Marguerite was astonished to see so many women moved by the nonchalance of James Dean.

The following year, one Tuesday in December, the telephone rang at four in the morning, waking Marguerite and her parents. Petrified by the insistent ringing that tore through the silence, they had all stared at the phone, as if hoping it was just a bad dream and they could go back to sleep. Finally her father had picked up the receiver, barking out staccato, impatient words. The two women remained silent in the face of this paternal outburst. He

21

ended the call crying out, 'Where is my daughter?' She would always remember the surreal, cold voice in which he told them that Hélène's car had skidded off the road, which was icy, and crashed into a tree. Her mother, whiter than her dressing gown, was shaking her head from left to right in denial of the facts. Marguerite said nothing. With an almost frightening calm, she had gone into her sister's room and buried herself beneath the duvet, as she had when they were little girls, lighting up their faces with a torch to frighten themselves during the night.

From that day her life began to shrink. The family that was left talked more quietly; their dreams were more modest. Their father would suppress anything that looked like joy. He had lost his oldest and beloved daughter. Happiness was taboo. They had suddenly become three instead of four, and had to learn to live with the absence that filled so much space. Years had passed, but the wound never healed.

She looks at the strange appliance Frédéric has given her. She doesn't understand how it works, but he assured her, 'You only have to press here and you'll get Radio Bonheur.' She often listens to Line Renaud, and songs that remind her of her youth. When she hears Guy Béart singing about the lilacs coming into flower again, she lets her tears flow.

. . .

Now her world has shrunk again. *Monday: cemetery. Tuesday, 10 a.m.: exercise class. Wednesday, 2 p.m.: Ludovic. Thursday: nothing. Friday, 4 p.m.: exercise class. Saturday: nothing. Sunday: nothing.* And once a month a visit to the museum with her senior discount card. At her age, you get asked to more funerals than dances.

4

It was the surprise he'd been searching for over the past few months. Leafing through a magazine, Marcel had noticed that there was to be a concert of Chaâbi music at the Algerian Cultural Centre in Paris, in the 15th arrondissement. He had seized the opportunity and got in touch with the group, asking them to play at his ruby wedding. All the guests had said that they would come along and help them celebrate. Their daughter, Manou, had been the first to respond, then their partners at the Scrabble Club, his colleagues at the zoo and Nora's at the mini-market where she worked, some of their neighbours, friends they hadn't seen in ages and cousins from afar who arrived the night before. Mattresses were piled up in several people's homes, and there were pillow fights between children now in their sixties.

. . .

Nora wore a long dress with a floral pattern, bought long ago in a market in Saint-Tropez. 'Don't you think it's a bit too much?' Marcel had asked at the time. 'A bit too much what? *Olé olé?*' she had replied. 'Remember you married an unpredictable woman. I can still surprise you.'

That summer they had gone from nightclub to nightclub, surrounded by tourists. Nora, beautiful in her brightly coloured dress, a glass of vodka and grapefruit juice in her hand, had smoked thin cigarettes with gilt paper.

Manou had found some old slides, which were being projected onto the white wall: her parents, aged nine, outside the village school; taken by surprise kissing in the car on their wedding day; Marcel playing dominoes in the Café des Amis; Nora emerging from the sea, radiant with joy; all three of them in the maternity ward at the hospital; their move from Vincennes to Maisons-Laffitte. 'And to finish on something beautiful,' she said, 'here's Papa's best friend: a muscular body and short legs, thick flaps of wrinkled grey skin, feet with only three toes, small ears and a horn. Hector the rhinoceros!' The whole company had exclaimed at each slide in turn. Happiness is noisier when it's shared.

Marcel had danced with his daughter, then hugged his wife and closed his eyes. He was back on the boat with

Nora's hand in his; she was smiling at him; she was his vital spark. Everyone was calling for a speech. It was Nora who took the floor. 'Forty years ago, on 5 June 1964, I said "yes" in front of the mayor. If anyone asked me that question again today . . .' She paused for effect, as actors do in the theatre, and the audience waited for her to continue.

'I like to get up early; he goes to bed late. In the evening he wears slippers, while I go about barefoot. He loves playing bowls; I like synchronised swimming. I'm quick-tempered; he's easy-going. When I'm too hot, he's putting on a polo neck. My favourite dish is *shakshuka* with peppers; he loves sweetbreads. He's still arranging his Scrabble tiles while I've made a word that will score triple points. On clear nights he's unfaithful to me with Vega, Electra, Izar, Maia, Sirrah and the rest of the stars. He dreams of going to America to get a closer view of them, but I don't speak English. All the same, ever since he first opened his window when I threw pebbles at it, I've been in love with this man, and I wouldn't exchange him for anyone else in the world.'

Applause had rung out across the town hall of Maisons-Laffitte. Nora then drank down two glasses of champagne in quick succession, but the bubbles made her melancholy, so she went up to the first floor to rest. On the stairway, she passed Monique, with whom she had played in Scrabble tournaments for as long as she could remember. Monique immediately noticed that Nora's eyes were full of tears, so she rushed to join her in the hallway.

'What's the matter?'

Nora took her friend's hand in hers and said, in her husky voice, 'Growing old depresses me. I can't bear to look at myself in the mirror. I hate the fact that we're going to have to cling to each other to survive into old age. I love him, of course I do. He's my rock; I feel protected when I'm with him. But how are we going to survive the shipwreck that's lying in wait for us?'

Monique had smiled.

'Wait and see – you'll turn the corner and then you can thumb your nose at time.'

'But suppose something happens to him?'

'Don't look on the dark side. Just enjoy every day as it comes.'

'You're right; let's dance. Don't tell Marcel what I said, please.'

'You can count on me. I'll always be there for you.'

They had gone home at three in the morning, too full of emotion to go to bed. After all the cheerful noise of the party, a peaceful silence reigned in their apartment. Marcel suggested a last glass of something in the sitting room, but Nora had already drunk enough, so they just sat on the sofa in the dark, running through the film of the evening.

'The next landmark is in ten years' time, our golden wedding anniversary. We could be a bit rusty by then.'

'How about we celebrate that anniversary by ourselves, just the two of us?'

'How about we don't wait another ten years?'

'A journey in the other direction.'

'Are you talking about our story?'

'What would you say to crossing the Mediterranean? We'd see the coast of Algeria coming closer instead of receding into the distance.'

'We've been lucky,' she says.

'You were the one who made us lucky. You came back.' Marcel looks at her and she does not look away. 'You're my first love and my last love, and that's all there is to it.'

5

Her steps take her first to Path C, Plot 12.

She always begins by tidying up the neighbouring grave. These days no one visits *Hermeline, died too young, sorely missed*. She sweeps up the leaves, removes the thick covering of grime on the garden gnome and rearranges the plastic flowers in the marble vase. Only then does she turn to her husband. It is here, under this imposing slab of granite, that he rests in his mahogany coffin, priced eight thousand euros, guaranteed insect-proof, according to the undertaker's brochure. The gravestone has now been carved and put in place.

Henri Delorme
1929–2014
Husband, father and much-respected notary
Director of the Philharmonic Society
of Maisons-Laffitte

She thinks a bench would have been a good idea, somewhere for her to rest her legs. She manages to sit down on the grave at Henri's feet. She has spent fifty years hearing him talk about the Philharmonic Society. Imprisoned in her red velour seat, in her taffeta, satin or silk evening dress, watching the conductor of the orchestra, she never thought of anything else but her pillow. The second movement, the third movement and then an encore. Years of recitals, Chopin and more Chopin. Twenty-four preludes, twenty-one nocturnes, seventeen waltzes, fifty-eight mazurkas, four ballades, sonatas and a funeral march. She'd heard them all. At first she had pretended to have a headache.

'I don't understand any of it,' she used to say.

'Chopin is not to be understood but absorbed, Maggy,' he had replied.

To get away from it all, she used to hum 'My Log Cabin in Canada' in her head. But as the pianist hammered away at the black and white keys, the picture of the cabin faded into the mist and she thought about her pillow once more.

She stands up now, cursing her arthritis, picks up the brush and the watering can, and puts them back in the shopping bag with the bunch of white and yellow flowers.

Suzanne Jacquet   *Ernest Jacquet*
1915–1983   *1913–1984*

You don't turn down an opportunity, Papa – that's what you always told me.

One evening he had come home from the office where he worked as a clerk, smiling. 'You've been invited to the thirtieth birthday party being given for Maître Delorme's son,' he'd told her. 'Henri is an intelligent young man; one day he'll take over the office on the Place du Maréchal-de-Lattre. His father is the most highly regarded notary in this part of Paris.'

It had all followed on quite naturally. A simple navy blue linen dress with a white collar had been ordered from the dressmaker. Her mother had given her precise instructions on how to behave at table, how she must listen without interrupting, and when the evening came, she had arranged her hair in a modest chignon, held tightly in place by clips that gave her a headache. No one had asked her opinion. She was twenty-two years old, and in 1959 young girls did whatever their parents told them to do.

What would have happened but for the black ice on the road and that fatal skid? She had dreamed of following in Hélène's footsteps and studying at a graphic-art studio or an art college. But the shock had been so severe that it stopped her in her tracks. The way her sister had come off the road now dictated the way she would go: forward, in a straight line. You don't turn down an opportunity, and she would have done anything to obliterate the uneasy expression she saw on her mother's face every time she wanted to go out for the evening.

Despite feeling like a pawn on a chessboard, she had thought Henri looked good in his grey suit that evening, with a lilac handkerchief tucked into his breast pocket. He was particularly fond of lilac. He was used to social small talk, and she admired his easy manner.

He had thought her perfect. There was a natural elegance to the way she wore her sober dress, with its starched collar buttoned up to her neck, and the court shoes with the fine strap that encircled her slim ankles. Her chignon highlighted the regular oval of her face and her large, grey eyes. She held herself straight and was reserved, the complete opposite to the kind of flighty girl who laughed too loudly in order to attract the young man's attention.

He had asked her to dance, and she had worked hard to hide her clumsiness. He liked to lead; she liked to be led. The seal was set on the next fifty-five years of their lives. She never complained. Her father had made his choice, and she had obeyed. After his death she had continued to play her part, to honour his wishes, and because she simply didn't know what else to do.

She bends down, clears a few twigs off the grey stone, picks up her shopping bag, walks away slowly and feels a little calmer.

Path S, Plot 17
Hélène Jacquet
1934–1957

Marguerite puts down her armful of flowers and notices that the dates have become slightly worn. On the neighbouring grave, she reads, for the thousandth time, the carved words *Time passes, memories live on.*

She is alone in cherishing their memories and their wild laughter now; she is the only one who remembers their family and their lost childhood. Her sister had given her a wonderful present for her twentieth birthday: a visit to Rome! They had decided not to tell anyone else about it, and she had felt a delicious shiver of excitement at the idea of this lie. Hélène had borrowed some money – she'd worry about how to pay it back later. Marguerite would see the Sistine Chapel, walk round the Coliseum, throw coins into the Trevi Fountain and make a wish. In their compartment on the sleeper train, they had stayed awake all night.

'Why have I never seen you flirting?' asked Hélène. 'Do you know how many lovers I've had? Twelve!'

Marguerite, overcome by this confession, had blushed, and murmured, 'I did kiss Louis Leduc in the playground.'

'I'm not talking about playground kisses; I'm talking about going to bed with someone. I haven't counted the number of people I've kissed among my twelve – that would be more like forty people.'

'Forty?!'

In the capital of *la dolce vita*, Marguerite had discovered another side to her sister. She rode her scooter too fast, drank Chianti and laughed heartily with the waiters at the trattorias. Hélène had always let them think she led the orderly life of a law student. In reality, Hélène had never registered with the university; instead she mixed with an easy-going crowd who lived life at a hundred miles an hour, speeding between Montmartre and Saint-Germain-des-Prés. It was a bohemian existence of nights with no tomorrow. She would turn up unannounced at Maisons-Laffitte, her bags full of crazily useless trinkets, and Marguerite secretly vowed infinite love towards this elder sister who was away from them too often. Yet it was Hélène who always held her close. The more reserved younger sister loved Hélène's great attachment to her. She needed it as she needed air to breathe.

On that December night Marguerite had suddenly become both the elder and the younger sister. All their parents' attention, all their worry, all their hopes were now added up and concentrated on her. The joy divided in two.

'My dear Hélène, life doesn't often turn out the way we imagined it. I thought you would be with me right to the end.'

Finally Marguerite goes back to Path C, Plot 12. She looks right and left, then whispers to Henri's gravestone, 'I hate Chopin.'

6

When they were seventy-two, they took part in the interclub competition in Nice for the first time. They had saved up banknotes and coins in a shoebox so that they could afford a room with a sea view.

In the coach on the way there, Marcel had watched Nora as she gesticulated while talking and he had thought how beautiful she was, with her expressive face and the crow's feet at the corners of her laughing eyes. He had first met her as a child, but the toll taken by the passing years had not affected his love for her one bit. Nora had begun to hum a tune from their old homeland, Algeria, and when Marcel had joined in the chorus, another man in the coach had exclaimed, 'That one always reminds me of my grandmother!' Listening to them, the other passengers began to clap their hands and smile. They knew the song too, and they allowed themselves to be lulled by the soft music made by this couple from another place.

. . .

When they arrived at the hotel, they had gone straight up to see the room they had chosen at the travel agency. She liked surprises; he preferred things to look exactly as they had in the hotel brochure. They sat on the bed to test the mattress and make sure it would be welcoming when they came in that evening to sleep.

There were shutters and Marcel liked that kind of thing, opening them to greet the dawn. They could see the sea from their French window, just beyond the Promenade des Anglais and the shingle beach, turning from grey to green under the rays of the sun. Sparkling. Perfect. He was sometimes jealous of Nora's love for the water and her wish to dive straight in, head first. He unpacked their suitcases, putting the red-and-blue swimsuit that she had bought for this occasion away in the wardrobe.

'It's a little too cold for bathing, my mermaid.'

'Swimming is never out of season, you softie.'

Nora put on a pretty embroidered blouse, and she laughed at Marcel's Bermuda shorts above his white calves.

At 7 p.m. they had sat down with their friends on a terrace facing the sea and, following the owner's advice, ordered grilled sea bass stuffed with fennel, washed down with a fruity Muscadet to celebrate the early arrival of spring. Their desserts took some time to arrive, night had fallen, and the women had put on their cardigans. They ordered another bottle of wine, and finished it at their leisure, laughing heartily, yet again, at Nora's account of the tournament when she had won a match with the word 'wizardry', thus gaining herself points and applause in equal measure.

Last year the Nice Scrabble Club had visited its opposite number in Maisons-Laffitte and had beaten them soundly, but this time Maisons-Laffitte intended to return home with the cup. For four days they would play one game in the morning and two in the afternoon. After that they would explore another cove, or the local countryside. And the pleasant ritual they were now enjoying would be repeated every evening. With a clumsy gesture, Marcel upset his glass and wine spilled over the table. It only made them laugh all the more. This little escapade, far from home, made them feel deliciously light-hearted.

They had returned to the hotel about eleven that night, and had opened the French windows so that they could breathe in the smell of the sea. She had killed a mosquito with their *Guide to Nice* and a tiny drop of blood had left a mark on the wall. They had fallen asleep quickly, tired after the coach journey, the wine they had drunk and the prospect of the following day.

Marcel had woken up unsure as to where he was after

this first night in unfamiliar surroundings. He had been dreaming of a star called Nora. He watched her get up, dress and pour him some orange juice before they both went out on to the balcony for breakfast. Crisp bread rolls, and lemon marmalade with crystallised peel in it, adding a final note of perfection. The sun, halfway between the sky and the sea, promised a beautiful day ahead of them.

On the stage, gold- and silver-plated cups awaited the winners, with lucky bags for the losers. Some of the games were still going on. At a desk, looking grave, stopwatch in hand, sat the judge who was presiding over this tournament, where over a hundred players were all earnestly trying to make the highest scoring word. Sitting at table number 23, Marcel's head was propped on his hands as he concentrated on finding the best combination for the letters on his tiles.

Nora had come over to whisper in his ear, 'I've finished. I'm not playing again until two, so I'm off for a swim.' He had made a vague gesture before immersing himself in his letters once more.

Nora felt good in her new swimsuit. At first she had chosen a two-piece, but she was a realist and had then decided that, at her age, the time for bikinis was over. At the other end of the beach, a father and child were flying a kite. It was low season and she loved having the sea to herself. The water was chilly but pleasant, and she had gone in with the confidence of a young girl. She had swum out as far as the floating platform, proud of her achievement. She'd come back out here tomorrow and this time she'd wave at Marcel.

When he had added an 'a', an 'r' and a 'y to 'comment', making a word of ten letters, he had raised his head to look for her, but then remembered that she had gone for a swim. She was always pleased for him when he did well, even if he was winning and she was losing. In bed this evening, they'd talk about the words that had gained them a triple score.

And then a man wearing a grey suit had appeared on the little stage set up for the prize-giving, holding a microphone.

'If Monsieur Marcel Guedj is in the hall, would he please go to the reception desk at his hotel as quickly as possible.'

Marcel didn't take in the words at first; then he stood up too suddenly, knocking his rack of letters and sending 'commentary' and all his other words flying. He ran the whole way along the Promenade des Anglais to the hotel. Seeing the navy blue uniforms at reception, he realised that something was very wrong. He felt dizzy. One hand on his heart, the other clutching the desk.

'We're so sorry, but your wife has had an accident.'

He would have liked an armoured steel door to prevent him from hearing the rest.

'It was a gentleman out walking who raised the alarm.'

They had chosen a restaurant. That evening they would dine together, drink wine, laugh, and the two of them would fall asleep curled up next to each other. Two spoons put in the drawer in their usual place.

'A heart attack.'

They were going back to Algeria for their golden wedding in three months' time. They had reserved a first-class cabin on the boat.

'Is she all right?'

On the way back on Wednesday, the coach was going to take a detour to show them the mediaeval village of Entrevaux perched against the mountainside. Hand in hand, they would cross the drawbridge, walk on the ramparts, visit the citadel and the cathedral.

'It was too late. There was nothing the emergency services could do.'

Marcel had raised his head to look at the police officer.

'I want to see her.'

7

Marguerite merges into the grey of the sky; only her white hair lightens her frail silhouette. She knows this part of town by heart, and she would have liked to have gone walking here with Henri. But he took his car everywhere, even to go to the Philharmonic Society's office, which was only three streets away. She still goes for a walk every day, as far as the racecourse, whatever the weather. 'It's ridiculous at your age; you'll get mugged,' her son keeps saying. *At your age.* It seems to be the only thing he can say. She knows that at seventy-eight she left her youth behind her long ago. People stand up for her on the bus, but she's still capable of crossing the road without having to take anyone's arm.

She no longer feels attractive; she is a twig, a feather, a mote of dust to be brushed away with the slightest gesture. Her knees play nasty tricks on her, and she fears the time when she won't be able to move so easily. So she slows down to match her new role. She is aware that she won't win this race; it's already been lost. Fighting back is useless, a vain ambition, even if she does go to gentle exercise classes twice a week to combat her stiffness.

Ever since she stopped doing voluntary work at the library, the days seem long. The arrival of digital technology, and of young Chloé, who climbed up and down the stepladder so easily, made her realise that it was time she gave up the job.

There's no need to hurry any more: no one is expecting her. Before Henri's death, she was invited to parties given by all the local bigwigs. She used to wear a pretty dress and the jewellery she was given for Christmas each year, but in between the petits fours and an Albinoni adagio she had nothing to say to her hosts. Dignified and impeccably turned out, as her husband demanded. Yet another tribute to his success, while all she really wanted to do was to feel light, to be quietly crazy, to eat three chocolate eclairs in a row, to walk bare-headed in the rain. She thinks of all the things she's never done. She is free now. But it's too late.

Perhaps she could ask Maria to go for a walk with her next time. She wraps herself up in her woollen coat, smiling sadly at the shop window that reflects a lonely old lady standing on the pavement. She remembers the day she bought it. She had wanted the salesgirl to know. 'This will be my last,' she'd said. Warm, not too pale a colour, it must do for other people's funerals. She rubs her neck against the fur of the collar, like a last caress.

Tomorrow she will see her grandson, the one ray of sunlight in her week. They are going to plant hyacinth bulbs together. She has learned about gardening from *Green Fingers* magazine. It's often the aphids and weeds that win. Then they'll make pancakes. There will be flour everywhere, and Ludo will look happy in his large apron and little chef's hat. She hopes he will sleep over in the blue bedroom. She will tuck him up in bed, talk to him about the flowers that will soon be in bloom, and watch as sleep overcomes him in the middle of the story she is telling. For his birthday, she's going to take him to the zoo; that's what he likes best.

She loves his spontaneity and his clumsiness. He hasn't inherited his father's severity, this man who tells her she ought to be in bed by eight o'clock, and that having dreams is inappropriate for a woman of seventy-eight. Last Wednesday Ludo asked what made her happy when she was little. She told him it was dancing with her sister in the sitting room. He wanted to do the same, so she chose a record and they whirled round before dropping onto the sofa cushions, completely out of breath. She would have loved to dance like that with a whole crowd of grandchildren, but life had decided otherwise.

Back at home, she admires the ranunculus flowers in a vase, displaying their colourful tutus. They remind her of the singer Line Renaud. She adores love songs that talk about sugar and honey, blue sky and the pale ocean. She hears a door open and turns round.

'Oh, there you are, Maria. Sit down and I'll make some coffee.'

'I can do that, Madame Delorme.'

'No, no, it will give me something to do.'

Maria is like part of the furniture, or rather she has been dusting it twice a week for thirty years. Small and sturdy, with a thick brown fringe sitting over her forehead, she looks like one of the Playmobil toys that Ludovic takes out of the cupboard when he comes to see her.

'Do you think I should get a dog?'

'Dogs leave hairs everywhere.'

'It would keep me company.'

'You need to give these things time.'

'I'm tired of leaving the house on my own, coming back on my own, talking to no one but myself in the middle of all my bits and pieces here. I don't even knit.'

'As I said, madame, you must let time take its course.'

Time. Routine. The empty twin bed. Sometimes she

misses her husband's voice. There's not a clearing of the throat, not a snore to break the silence, no second used cup in the sink. From now on she can read Françoise Sagan without hiding her book; she can listen to Line Renaud on a continuous loop, and even do a little dance, sometimes, on the oriental rug in front of the fireplace. Last week she cleared out one of Henri's wardrobes: his three-piece suits and his ties. Next time she will deal with his shoes. There is a half-empty coat rack in the hall, and on her index finger, a wedding ring: traces of her previous life.

These last few years he had developed a passionate interest in the Napoleonic Wars. While he read, she would admire the roses, sitting on the garden bench under the intimate light of the moon. Between them it wasn't war, nor was it boredom. There was something permanent about the relationship that reassured her. He would remain beside her to the end, a rug over his knees, the light on, his magnifying glass in his hand, concentrating on *The Battle of Austerlitz*.

Christmas will soon be here. A Christmas tree for one? Her life has no meaning any more.

'Never mind the silver, Maria. Come and sit down with me – the coffee's ready.'

'Yes, madame, and then I'll go and bring the washing in.'

A slight silence falls between the two women; then Maria breaks it.

'Did you see all those terrible disasters on TV? That hurricane in Argentina, destroying whole villages – it's dreadful.'

'You're right, and I shouldn't complain. I have a house, a garden, a plot reserved for me in the cemetery next to my husband. I'm not ill; I have all the insurance I need; I've had my flu injection. I have a good family doctor, and money; I don't put too much salt in my food; I don't smoke or drink; I go to bed early. So what can happen to me?'

'It's wonderful. You'll live to be a hundred.'

'You really think so? That sounds awful!'

Automatically she opens the post: some bills and concert tickets.

'Here, Maria, for you. There are two tickets – you can take a friend.'

'Oh no, madame. That's too much.'

'No, not at all – you go and have a nice time, or I'll simply be throwing them away. Next Tuesday you can choose a dress from my wardrobe and a piece of jewellery to wear with it. You'll be the most beautiful member of the audience listening to Chopin.'

'You're so kind.'

'You can go home now – the washing can wait until tomorrow. See you then, Maria.'

She bends down to pick up a coat hanger from the floor, makes a face, rubs her hip. She'll have to talk to Dr Dubois about that. She leaves the coat hanger where it is; she'll put it away later. The compensation for solitude is that you can do what you want whenever you want. All those dresses and suits, sorted by colour and the seasons! What do the seasons matter to her now? Henri is looking at her from his silver frame. She moves the photo of her sister, who is smiling mischievously, and puts it in front of her husband, his expression too serious.

Five in the afternoon, the twilight hour. The day takes its leave; the sitting room fills with shadows. She hesitates: should she stay in the dark or switch on all the lights? A hot bath, an omelette, half a chapter of her book, something on TV, and tomorrow Ludo will be here. It's the time when Radio Bonheur broadcasts advertisements: *Tuesday from two to four p.m., bingo with Father Jean-Jacques, three euros a ticket, eight euros for three. There will be many prizes, cakes and hot drinks. Sunday the twenty-second, afternoon dance organised by the veterans in the town hall, coffee, chocolate, bar, free entrance. Retired gentleman, likes philosophical discussions, walking and the good life, offers escape to a cultivated lady, driving licence essential . . .*

. . .

What would she do with a man? She hadn't succeeded in taming Henri. And anyway, she doesn't have a driving licence.

8

Not a day goes by when he doesn't relive his frantic run
from the hotel to the beach all over again. Nora's large,
open, empty eyes, the fixed expression on her face. And
all the people out walking, coming over to get a closer
look at death.

He came home alone to the apartment that they had
left together a few days before, his civil status now
changed.

He brought back their suitcase. And the red-and-
blue swimsuit, handed over to him in a plastic bag by
a member of staff at the mortuary. The suitcase is still
closed. He has put the swimsuit away in the wardrobe,
along with Nora's raffia handbag. On the third shelf to
the left.

He has hidden his Scrabble set behind the encyclo-
paedias in the library, and has torn the *Guide to Nice* to

shreds, as if getting rid of something that brought bad luck. First the page about Entrevaux, then all the others.

Now the sink is full of unwashed dishes, rubbish is piling up on the balcony, and the photograph albums lie open on the table. He uses her shampoo to recapture the scent of her hair. Several times a week. He buys tulips from her florist and arranges them in the blue vase that she liked. He sits there in front of the flowers, waiting for the moment when they will open. He gets up, adds a few drops of water to the vase, sits down in front of them again, dazed. They are too beautiful for a man on his own.

The doctor has told him about the seven stages of mourning. Stage three is anger; it often comes back. So does helplessness. There is no order to it; it's all random. All it takes is for him to hear a song on the radio, to come upon one of her sandals with a few grains of sand still sticking to it and the memories come flooding in, uninvited. On bad days all seven stages dance a crazy saraband in his head. His hair has turned white over-night, in contrast to his bushy eyebrows, which are still black.

He would have liked her to be buried at Mouzaïa, near the hills where he had seen her for the first time. Her skin soft, wearing shorts and a skimpy T-shirt, the new neighbour, Nora, had thrown pebbles at the shutters of his room. She had hypnotised him with her shining black eyes, her complexion like that of a ripe peach, her bold smile. That was where they had raced down the hillsides and gorged themselves on the figs that fell from the trees.

His daughter didn't know their Algeria and she wanted to be able to visit her mother's grave, so the Maisons-Laffitte Cemetery was perfect for that. He couldn't summon up the courage to fight. He had agreed, but on two conditions: Nora was to be embalmed, and when his time came, he would lie beside his wife, their names carved one below the other. He hadn't set foot in the cemetery since the funeral. Except once, on All Saints' Day, when Manou had insisted on it. There was no bench to sit on, and he had stumbled over a forgotten watering can. All those mourners trudging along the paths depressed him. He wanted to lie down beside her, but you had to put on a brave face amid all this sadness.

Not a day goes by when he doesn't tell himself that he should have gone with her, instead of keeping his eyes riveted on words that might score him a double.

He turns down the offer of sleeping tablets. He doesn't want to be anaesthetised. If he feels bad, it means she's still there. When he ends up falling asleep at dawn, he dreams of her kisses. He wakes up and the unbearable reality hits him with full force. The two of them: the mingled threads of a precious fabric woven day after day. Abruptly torn apart. He can't get used to it. He can only bury his head in the pillow next to his and try to catch the honeyed scent that has long disappeared.

'Help me, Nora. I can't manage any more.'

Not a single day of the last year has gone by when he doesn't see that room in Nice, the room where he fell asleep in her arms without losing himself.

Nothing has been moved in the apartment, but everything is different. He paces up and down, stopping each time in front a calendar that seems to be stuck on 25 March 2014. The metronome has changed its rhythm. Marcel has been catapulted into another world. A joyless world, without arguments, without lunches for the three of them, Manou included. He's afraid of answering the telephone in case it's that friend of Nora's, a widow herself, who keeps inviting him over to dinner. He has stopped answering his post. All those messages of condolence just make him mad: *You must master your loss. Time softens the pain. A time will come, you'll see, when the love of life will come back to you. It will be all right.* No, it will not be all right.

. . .

Not a single day of the year when he hasn't seen her, bursting with laughter, in a second-hand photo frame on the chest of drawers in the sitting room.

He must pay his bills, clean his shoes, empty a drawer full of mementoes. His daughter gives him homework, just as she hands it out to the children in her class. She has warned him, smiling, 'You'll get your report next month.' But he wants to be unhappy in his own way. Over the sweetbreads with vegetables that she has cooked, a conversation begins.

'Have you been to see Hector?'

'He's getting old.'

Manou puts her hand on her father's shoulder. Marcel jumps; he's not used to being touched these days, however lightly.

'Suppose I came to live on the fourth floor here, so that I could look after you? There's an apartment becoming vacant. I could cook for you.'

He doesn't reply.

'Aren't you going to go back to the Scrabble Club?'

'I'll never play Scrabble again. Scrabble kills!'

'There are games of rummy organised every Friday at the senior citizens' club.'

'And I suppose the next step is the old folks' home?'

'Maman wouldn't have wanted to see you going round and round like that rhino in his enclosure.'

'Leave Maman out of this.'

Marcel gets up and looks out of the window. He can't talk about Nora. Not to his daughter, or to their friends. Not to anyone.

'Why don't you come and tell my pupils about the stars? Make them dream.'

'Maybe I will. We'll see.'

She opens her bag and takes out an envelope. 'This is for you . . . a present.'

'I don't need anything.'

'I'm giving you a course of seawater therapy at Saint-Malo.'

'Why not a stay in hospital while you're about it? I'm never going on holiday to the seaside again – I've already told you that.'

'Think about it. Take your time.'

He puts the envelope on the table, picks up his coat and leaves.

This is his refuge. He walks as if Nora might come round the corner of a path, smiling, and ask, 'How are the antelopes doing?' He goes down past the reptiles, then past the tortoises. They are nestling close together, shell against shell, under an artificial sun. That's what he needs, apart from the shell. His walk always ends in the same place. On the bench opposite the rhino. Hector seems to be frozen in time.

Do rhinoceroses cry when they lose their mate?

The warning sounds for closing time. Late visitors pass through the large barred gate; he will be the last. He hurries past the window of the travel agency. Everything had been so well organised. The tour of Spain with a caravan: the hills of Bilbao, Barcelona in her arms, castanets and her flowery dress in Seville. Life keeps some nasty surprises up its sleeve.

In the streets, people are happily enjoying the balmy air they have missed so much during the winter. Marcel goes into a bistro, orders a coffee, hesitates at the counter, then sits down at a table. He looks at his large, wrinkled hands. No longer do they caress anyone, embrace anyone. Dead branches covered in flowers from the cemetery: a pretty metaphor, but without an escape. He rubs his hands together to warm himself up. On his own, he is vegetating. He needs to be half of a couple, and it's the other half that keeps him anchored.

The waiter brings his coffee. He drinks several mouthfuls and notices that the cup is trembling slightly. He puts it down. All those years to come, without her.

. . .

Not a day passes when he doesn't kiss her postcard: *I'm coming back. I miss Vincennes. And that's not the only thing I miss. Nora.*

Not a single day.

9

'Another one knocking on your door.'

'I don't understand.'

'Another widow, another amputee. I suppose that's rather a strong term to use, but I'm telling you that's what it feels like to me – an amputation. Seven months later and I still find myself in tears, alone in my bed, arms dangling and staring into space. Is that normal, Doctor?'

Dr Dubois. A dry man with glasses, who takes the time to listen to his patients. She has known him for ever. As a young doctor, he diagnosed Frédéric's chicken-pox then, over the course of the years, Henri's prostate trouble, her own menopausal symptoms and Maria's varicose veins. They have grown old together.

'I know what you mean. One in every two widows asks me for a crutch.'

'A crutch?'

'You won't be needing that.'

'Well, no. I still go for a walk every day.'

'That's not what I mean. Some people need a mild antidepressant.'

'Can it be managed without? Do you think I'm strong enough to stand up to the storm? Sometimes I feel as if I'm like that song – I'm nothing but a shadow going from the window to my chair. Do you think I still exist? Forgive me for all this soul-searching, Doctor, but I get so afraid sometimes, afraid that I won't be able to cope, and I daren't talk about it to my son.'

He looks at her, smiling. For years and years he has watched her playing her part as the notary's wife, beautiful, straight-backed, her make-up perfect.

'You must look after yourself now.'

'Myself?'

'What if I prescribed you a course of thermal therapy at a spa? Bagnères-de-Bigorre in the Pyrenees.'

She likes the name; it sounds almost exotic.

'The course is called "The Secrets of Youth". It's mostly jacuzzis and massages, and they'll wrap you in seaweed and mud.'

'Isn't that rather old-fashioned?'

'Far from it. Such things are all the rage again these days.'

'Thank you, Doctor. I'll consider it, but I don't think it's my kind of thing. I'm not very up to date.'

'And how is Ludovic?'

'Growing up. He's nearly eight. You were talking about a crutch, Doctor. He's mine.'

She leaves the doctor's consulting room; the town is bathed in a warm light. This is the kind of April sunshine she loves because it warms her old bones. For the first time since 23 September last year, she walks with a lighter step. It may not be the mild spring air that is giving her this sense of freedom. And why not be spontaneous, since her husband is no longer here to shut her up like a curio in a glass case?

But where will she find the energy for the journey? Henri used to see to everything. Always. And she won't know anyone. She slows down. It takes courage to leave a home, knowing that when you return, no one will ask you anything about it. And there is one last, delicate hurdle to be negotiated. She prepares for the phone call to her son as if she were about to sit an exam. Is she always to be this little girl faced with all these men?

She takes a deep breath and dials the number.

'Hello, darling. Guess what I'm going to do?'

'What are you saying?'

'I've just been to see Dr Dubois.'

'What's wrong? Do you have to go to hospital?'

'He said I should have a course of thermal therapy. At the Bagnères-de-Bigorre spa in the Pyrenees.'

Frédéric wonders if his father, who hated mineral water, would have approved of his mother going to a spa.

'But suppose someone burgles the house while you're away at the back of beyond?'

'No, no. No one will burgle the house, and anyway, I'm going to ask Maria to stay here for a few nights—'

'Let me stop you right there! Surely you're not going to pay Maria to sleep in our house! I've been telling you for months to install a security camera. I've seen an ad for one. I'll sort it out.'

'I don't need to be watched.'

'You never know who you might meet at a place like that. And suppose you fall ill. Who's going to come and get you from eight hundred metres above sea level?'

'I'm not going to climb Mont Blanc.'

'You've never liked the peaks.'

'It's never too late, and you're getting mixed up. It was your father who didn't like mountains. He adored the châteaux of the Loire, so we went to visit them for thirty-two years running. I know every square centimetre by heart – Plessis-lèz-Tours, de Montsoreau—'

'And how are you going to get to Bagnères-de-What's-Its-Name?'

She looks at the tall trees at the end of the garden.

'Do you think the mountains are dangerous at my age?'

'Yes, Maman. If you like, Carole and I will take you to the botanical gardens. It will do you good, and it's much cheaper.'

And that is where the conversation ended. She looks at her bookshelves. Not long after Henri's death, she put *Madame Bovary* on display. Hélène was the one who had given her the book, mentioning, with a smile, that some of the passages were considered immoral and had been much criticised. Marguerite hadn't understood what could be so shocking about the scene in the carriage – street names passing by, galloping horses. But a few pages further on, feeling uneasy, she had stopped reading, for fear of finding out more. The bookmark was still there where she had left it. *And Emma returned home more inflamed, more avid than ever.* Marguerite's numb body trembles. An unknown warmth creeps into the pit of her stomach; she hesitates. Yes, another few lines; today she wants to know. *She would undress brutally, pulling at the thin lace of her corset, which would fall about her hips like a sliding serpent.* She closes the book, her cheeks burning, her eyes looking into space; she strokes the cover, then carefully places the book back between *Napoleon the Hero* and *The Civil Code of France.*

Early the next day she wakes her son.

'I've made up my mind. I'm going to Bagnères-de-Bigorre.'

'On your own head be it.'

She puts down the phone, goes up to her bedroom and spreads all her clothes out across the bed. She feels like a little girl of ten, about to leave home for the first time. The doorbell rings. She has forgotten that it's Tuesday.

'Hello, Maria. I'm so glad to see you. What would you take if you were going away to a spa?'

'Are you unwell?'

'Apparently I have to look after myself. I'm going to Bagnères-de-Bigorre.'

'I don't know it.'

'Listen, I thought perhaps you might come and stay in the house while I'm away?'

'But, madame . . .'

'Think of it as a holiday. You could enjoy the garden.'

'Oh, thank you.'

'Excuse me, Maria, but I have an important phone call to make.'

'And I have to get on with my work.'

Maria irons Marguerite's flannelette nightdress. She thinks of her studio flat, thirty metres square. Rose bushes and freshly mown grass. It's a tempting proposition.

· · ·

Contrary to habit, Marguerite pours herself a second cup of tea. She feverishly searches for the number in her notebook.

'Hello, Doctor. I'm sorry to phone so early.'

'You're certainly an early bird.'

'It's about the thermal therapy.'

'Have you changed your mind?'

'Yes, but I've no idea what to expect. Do you think I should buy a tracksuit? And what about the evenings? Something more formal, or do people dress casually? And I can't swim – is that a problem? I hope all the masseurs are women? I read a magazine article that said—'

'Don't worry, Madame Delorme. Everything will be fine. When do you want to leave?'

'As soon as possible.'

Everything is ready: her suitcase, her handbag, a small case containing her medication. Out of breath, Marguerite sits down on her bed. Tomorrow she will go to Lili's and buy a dressing gown, and she'll go to the hairdresser's for a shampoo-and-set, and get a manicure. She wants to look perfect if she's going to be spoiled. And then she will go to the bookshop to get something amusing to read. She'll tell the salesgirl it's for a journey by train.

10

It all reminds him of the advertisements for hearing aids and absorbent pads that have been inundating his letterbox ever since he turned seventy. He hates the mud and the seaweed, the obligatory bath cap makes him itch, the ridiculous flip-flops that are too large, and he almost slipped on the tiled floor between the shower and the washbasin. Everywhere there's either an oppressive silence or the unbearable sound of water running or dripping. And not so much as a chocolate in the fruit basket to sweeten his stay here. The meticulously timed schedule makes him feel aggressive. No chance of a lie-in, no time to switch on the radio and listen to the news from around the world when he wakes up.

And these old people, with their white towelling bathrobes, haunting the corridors like ghosts with glasses of water in their hands, they're too much for him. 'The Secrets of Youth' – I ask you! The average age is seventy-five! And then there's the question that everyone asks everyone else: 'Did you have a good night?' It's come full circle; they've turned back into babies whose sleep is easily disturbed.

An old lady with a mauve-tinted poodle perm accosted him. 'I'm looking for a platonic relationship with an octogenarian. Are you interested?' Feeling cowardly, he turned his head away. He'd like to be with Nora, in their hills or in a corner of paradise, if paradise exists. He had a hard-on one morning. Who for? Why? There's no one for him to caress by his side. It is a punishment on top of the punishment he's already suffered. One of the thousand pieces of collateral damage linked to that one essential loss.

Just a moment ago a trainee male nurse called him 'grandpa'. Why not 'dinosaur', he thought, while you're about it? He knows that he shows symptoms of old age, but he doesn't want to join the club just yet. He avoids draughts, cold weather is bad for his arthritis, and the fear of some new disaster makes him sensitive to life. He wears several layers of sweaters, and an extra short-sleeved shirt under them, just in case. Old age means shivering a bit too.

He can't bear being shut in by four walls, being surrounded by faces that will never be smooth again in spite of all the creams and the exfoliation. He'd have preferred to go for a walk. He didn't want to be a calf among other calves, made to drink water and swallow herbal tea made from St John's wort.

Nine a.m.: a hot shower followed by an ice-cold shower. Ten a.m.: immersion in a jacuzzi up to his neck. Eleven a.m.: a shower massage. Lying on his stomach, he feels hot thermal water raining down on his back and legs. They say it's particularly good for insomnia. He doesn't want to treat his insomnia. Twelve noon: 'You're tense up here on your back. Relax – you're full of knots. I see you have dry skin. I'd advise using a moisturising lotion.' She's the one with hands as rough as sandpaper. Without something sweet in the morning his blood sugar gets low, and his morale is in free fall. He should have brought some chocolate biscuits with him. He could have hidden them in his wardrobe and eaten them one by one, like a sad little boy.

This spa was a very bad idea, but he hadn't been able to summon up the arguments to decline it. Nora had been the one who held the three of them together. When Manou suggested coming to live on the fourth floor of the same building as him, an octopus had thrown a tentacle round his neck, strangling his words. He doesn't want to be one of a couple with his daughter. He wants his wife back.

'Hello. It's me.'

'Papa?'

'I don't need all this nonsense.'

'Don't be so childish. Are you eating well at least?'

'Today we're having cream of asparagus. It's a different soup every day. You know I don't like this kind of thing . . . and the mountains drive me nuts!'

'You never did appreciate the surprises I gave you when I was little. I used to find them hidden in your desk drawer.'

'But, darling—'

'You're staying on at Bagnères-de-Bigorre. A present is a present.'

11

'You're in room 207, on the second floor. Have you been here before?'

'No, this is my first time,' Marguerite replies, with a shy smile.

'It's relatively quiet at the moment. You'll be well looked after.' The receptionist gives her a magnetic card. 'Here's your key.'

Marguerite is baffled by the piece of white plastic.

'Don't worry, the young man here will go up with you.'

She would rather have had a traditional set of keys, but you have to move with the times. She was right not to listen to Frédéric, who has been bothering her with good advice for the last week. She has also been given soft towels and a pair of non-slip sandals. Nothing bad can happen to her here.

In her room, by way of welcome, there's a tray of

fruit, a bottle of mineral water and a padded basket full of body-care products. Before even unpacking her case, she opens the window wide and draws the dry, cold air deep into her lungs. The distant valley and its model-train landscape of wooden chalets and miniature cows remind her of the last time she stayed in the mountains, when she went away on a holiday camp. She was twelve years old. Marguerite takes off her shoes and walks over the thick, peach-coloured carpet, relieved to be barefoot again after that long journey. The train was crowded – trains always were these days. No one would have ventured to have such an intriguing colour as peach in the Delorme household, where the walls were always bland, invariably repainted with matt, smooth, soporific ivory every five years. She is worried about the bed, which is far too large for her, with all those pillows, bolsters and oversized cushions. She could be a character in *Snow White*.

It's time to phone her son. She picks up the receiver and taps the keys. Then she taps them again. Still no ringtone. Another complicated thing that she doesn't understand. She slams the door shut behind her, realises that she ought to have put a cardigan around her shoulders and discovers she has left the magnetic card inside the room. A locked door in an empty corridor: she is close to tears. Frédéric was right. It was crazy to have come here on her own, to this melancholy place, surrounded by mountains. She takes a few deep breaths, heads towards the lift, then explains her dilemma to the first person she meets.

'You have to put the card in the door, take it out again and then turn the handle.'

The woman's charming smile is a comfort.

'I'm afraid I left it on the bedside table in the room.'

'Go back to reception. They're very nice — they can make you a duplicate of your key. I mean that bit of plastic . . . The fact is, I'll never get used to it either!'

She doesn't feel brave enough to have dinner in the dining room. Too many new things in one day; all she really wants to do right now is slip between those starched sheets. She leans the largest pillow up against the wall behind her, then presses the switch on the bedside lamp. All the lights come on or go off at the same time. She gives up the idea of reading and instead lies back in the black night of Bagnères-de-Bigorre with her eyes open.

She wakes up with her head at an odd angle and looks blankly at all the pillows scattered over the floor. Then she remembers throwing them out one by one. Her first massage is at nine and she isn't ready; she won't even have time to have any breakfast. She doesn't like the white bathrobe hanging in the bathroom; she'd rather wear the one she chose at Lili's. Wrapped in lilac velour, she feels almost safe. She nibbles a biscuit that she picked up on the train, and munches part of an apple taken from the fruit platter.

In cubicle 12, a chubby-cheeked physiotherapist is waiting with a smile straight out of a brochure.

'Good morning, Madame Delorme. I'll be looking after you today. My name is Agnès. I hope your first night with us was a pleasant one.'

Marguerite slowly undresses, disliking the idea of exposing her wrinkled body to this youthful figure, all curves and shining vitality.

'We'll have to fatten you up a bit.'

Marguerite senses the kindness under the slightly harsh tone. 'My husband never wanted me to put on a single gram. I still take the same dress size as I did when I was eighteen.'

She knows she has lost weight; she skips meals so she doesn't have to sit down to eat by herself. Although her legs are still attractive, her skin has slackened here and there, particularly under her arms. And then there are her hands, which are more crumpled than a badly ironed sheet.

'Lean on me – I'll help you. Now, lie on your tummy, relax and let me pamper you.'

Agnès is discreet; she doesn't ask questions. Lying on the massage table, Marguerite is surprised to find herself letting go, entrusting herself to the warm hands that touch, feel and knead her. An hour later she stands up and staggers forward, feeling light-headed and outside time. In the corridors, bathrobes swish past each other in a strange, soft harmony. The peach-coloured carpeting that muffles sound is everywhere. She feels dizzy and looks at her feet. She has left her slippers in the cubicle.

In the ladies', she drinks a third glass of water in small sips. It's a rule the guests are told on arrival: a minimum of eight glasses of water a day. She wants to go to the toilet, but she needs to turn up at the cold shower, a reinvigorating tonic, in five minutes' time.

She has been sleeping poorly ever since Henri's death. She had become used to his snoring, just as some people get used to a train passing their windows at three in the morning. How does fate decide to shoot its arrows? Why aim at a small municipality in the suburbs of Paris and not towards Lake Geneva, or a street in Naples? In all those years of marriage she has never questioned herself. Here in Bagnères-de-Bigorre, somewhere between the seaweed and Agnès's hands, between three showers and a massage with hot stones, she takes time, for once, to rewind the film of her life. Did she love her husband? She remembers the majestic façade of the Château de Chambord. Why did she never tell him that she would have liked to go somewhere else for a change, not just the châteaux of the Loire every single year? She had been dignified and perfectly behaved. A good girl, such a good girl. Being coy doesn't excuse all those silences, but we each do our best with what we've been given. She has only ever been someone's daughter, someone's sister, someone's wife.

Facing the large window with its view of the mountains, she feels dizzy at the way her life has turned out. She hasn't had a real conversation with anyone since her arrival. Only 'thank you's, 'good morning's, 'goodbye's. Perhaps that is what she needs in order to make progress. It was a good decision to come here after all. Even if it is difficult, this project is doing her good. She thinks of Ludovic and the little huts he builds using cushions on the sofa; she thinks of their games of draughts. When she gets back, she'll tell him all about the funny swimming pools here, the interminable showers and the slices of rye bread without any butter. And he will tell her about his hiding places in the playground.

At seven in the evening she is to go to the main hall for a 'mid-race assessment'. It's a funny way to describe it, when most of the people here walk so slowly. The little woman with short hair whom she met outside the lift sits down beside her.

'My name is Paulette, I've been coming here for

twelve years, and it's always a pleasure. You'll see, you'll make a lot of friends from one stay to the next.'

The man in charge speaks up. 'Good evening, all of you, and thank you for choosing our course, "The Secrets of Youth". You should already be feeling the benefits of a change of rhythm and air. Pleasant surroundings, comforting care and a well-balanced diet are ideal for restoring your sense of inner harmony.'

The residents seem to be used to discussing their aches and pains without any embarrassment. Looking lost, two old men clutching their walking frames ask if someone can go out into the garden with them. A deep voice calls out from the back of the room.

'Can I order a cappuccino anywhere in this place?'

'No, monsieur. No caffeine and no alcohol. You have come here to the mountains with only one thing in mind: your health. Now, let me remind you all of the various activities we shall be offering you this evening: group relaxation therapy, posture training, a nutrition studio, a talk on how to prevent osteoporosis and how to manage incontinence.'

A chair falls over. Everyone turns to look as a tall figure leaves the room.

12

Could ridicule be fatal? Lying on treatment tables, the spa guests wrapped in hot, damp sheets look like mummies. The smell of clay tickles Marcel's nostrils, and he can think of only one thing: the fact that he needs a handkerchief. To his right, a lookalike for the Michelin man is snoring. He turns his head towards his neighbour on the left.

'Any idea when they're going to set us free?'

'They said after thirty minutes.'

'Thirty minutes of this! I'll never survive. My brain is having palpitations.'

'And my eyelid is jumping all over the place.'

'It's sheer torture. The silence gets on my nerves instead of calming me down!'

'Think about something else.'

'I can't. I have pins and needles in my toes.'

The Michelin man is snoring louder than ever.

'Are you sure this thermal therapy is right for you?'

'It was my daughter's idea.'

The bell goes for the end of the session. Two hydro-therapists release them and suggest a twenty-five-minute rest. Even their free time is strictly controlled. If Nora were here, it would be different. He wants to get away from these spotless white tiles. There are arrows pointing the way to the terrace with the panoramic view. Nothing is left to chance in this place.

The magnificence of the landscape finally gives him a sense of freedom. He has always needed the long view to feel good. Most of the residents are enjoying the last rays of the sun before it is swallowed up by the Pyrenees. In April the beautiful light is careful about the hours it keeps, and everyone wants to take full advantage. A group of quiet men is discussing the most recent ascent of the Col d'Aspin. A man who has left the age of twenty far behind him is clinging to the arm of a female care assistant. A little way off, a thoughtful husband is spreading a rug over his wife's legs.

There is still one empty deckchair left beside a frail figure wrapped in a shawl. The others have all been taken. The fragile woman looks lost in the middle of the orange canvas. Her hair is perfectly groomed; it's hard to believe that she has spent all day in the humid atmosphere. With a glass of spring water in her hand,

and a book on her knees, she is gazing at a distant village on the hillside.

'Is this chair free?' Without waiting for an answer, Marcel sits down. 'Did you hear a crack?'

'What kind of crack?' she asks without looking at him.

'The canvas giving way. These deckchairs are always too small for me.'

She remains motionless, staring at the landscape.

'Is this your first time here?' asks Marcel. 'I was given a course of seawater therapy in Saint-Malo, but I traded it in for this one. How about you?'

'My doctor said I needed a change of air. He was right too. The sky's so blue here.'

'Blue bores me. I like starry skies.'

'I've always preferred day to night.'

Not many words are exchanged. Scraps of conversation behind them punctuate the silence: 'On Monday we went to Lourdes. I brought back two bottles of holy water for my sister.'

'I expect you like the sun.'

'My son says it's not recommended at my age.'

'We're not going to get any younger; all the clay in the world won't change that. I hate all those bandages!'

'I liked the session with the sprinkler.'

'Yesterday afternoon? I thought that was a nightmare.'

'Do you think so? When I closed my eyes and felt a light shower across my shoulders, I really relaxed.'

'I sat cross-legged, like a frog on a water-lily leaf. When the torrent hit my head, I felt as if they were trying to wash me into the pond.'

'A frog?' With her hand to her mouth, she lets a little laugh escape.

'More like a toad!'

She laughs even louder, and he is surprised to hear the laughter of a little girl coming from an old lady's body.

'A toad wearing flip-flops!'

'Those horrible plastic things they make us wear.'

'Gene Kelly in *Singing in the Rain*.'

'Cyd Charisse in an emerald-green basque.'

'Her long legs like a tree frog's.'

'Oh, it's been so long!' she gasps.

'Since what? Tell me.'

'Since I laughed like that.'

'It makes me feel good too.'

Marcel steadies his breathing. He would like to offer his neighbour a pastis, but this place is too prim and proper for any chance of an aperitif. The conversations around them have died down. A light mist is rising from the valley.

'My daughter calls me every evening to find out if I'm eating properly.'

'My son does that too. He worries about me. He's

afraid I might break my hip or meet the wrong kind of person.'

'Do you have grandchildren?'

'Only one, sad to say, but he's a darling. How about you?'

'I have twenty-five, or rather my daughter, Manou, has twenty-five children in her class. She's a teacher.'

'I would have liked to be a teacher. My son is a notary.'

An announcement tells them that the terrace will close in fifteen minutes' time and that the light therapy is about to begin.

'Our time isn't our own here. They're always telling us where to go in this sanatorium.'

'Maybe, but I don't mind. I lost my husband seven months ago and I've been going round in circles ever since. I need someone to tell me where to go for a few days.'

She draws her shawl more closely around her body, which seems so fragile, as if regretting the confession of her recent bereavement. The beautiful evening light floods the terrace for a few moments more, then gives way to cold air that will soon make the mountains seem more disturbing.

'The light therapy on Tuesday did me good. Are you coming?'

He growls, 'No. I don't like artificial light. I think I'll go for a third carrot-and-cucumber juice.'

'As you wish.'

He watches her walking away. Her tightly twisted chignon, held in place by a great many invisible hairpins, doesn't let a single lock of hair escape.

13

'Hello, darling. How are you?'

'I'm not at all pleased with you.'

'Well, do say hello first, and then you can ask how my knees are doing. I'll tell you anyway: they're getting better and better.'

'Maman, I went by the house. Maria has moved in. Did you know she's sleeping in your bedroom? She was even wearing one of your dresses.'

'We'll talk about this later.'

'I'm not at all happy.'

'But, darling—'

'She's your cleaning lady! She's not from our circles, and there she is, sleeping in your sheets.'

'Maybe it's time we opened up our circles to other people.'

'The mountains can't be agreeing with you. I hope

you're not doing anything dangerous? Are you sure everything's included in the price? No extras?'

'Yes, some extra oxygen, a wider view. I'm going to hang up now: I must get ready for dinner. It's kind of you to worry about me.'

'Do be careful. Mind you don't slip on anything. I'll call at six tomorrow evening, so stay beside the telephone.'

In his dark office, Frédéric nervously bites the left-hand side of his lower lip. Since she became a widow, his mother has been unmanageable. 'Some extra oxygen!' It could be the first signs of dementia. He ought to mention it to Dr Dubois. And, really, he ought to have persuaded her to take a mobile phone. Then he'd be able to call her at any time. Without her husband to guide her, left to her own devices, she could do anything. Between two cases, his father had once told him, 'I've loved your mother, if not always well enough. She's a one-man woman; when I'm no longer around, it will be a complete disaster.' Maybe he ought to go to this spa. But the Duvernois estate and the Chassy de Montrachet sale entailing the purchase of a life annuity await him. She's expected back on Monday; he'll meet her at the station and there'll be no more going out after dark for her. As for Maria, he'll fire her. She looked grotesque in his mother's dress. He hates anything unexpected. One day, and only for that one day, he did try a new style, but he had felt ridiculous in front of his employees, in jeans and a sports shirt. He'd immediately gone back to wearing a suit, even at weekends. He had never seen his father in shirtsleeves; even on holiday, there could be no sartorial sloppiness. Fanciful notions are not his thing, and it's reassuring for Carole to have a well-groomed man beside her. The only way he lets off steam is by playing ping-pong on Sunday mornings with the Sartrouville team. Next week he'll call a firm that specialises in finding ladies' companions. Whatever it costs, it might enable him to limit the damage. He's an only son: there's no one else to keep things in line and as his father would have wanted. Maître Delorme: like father, like son. Yes, his father would be proud of him.

Marguerite is looking out of the window. The terrace is deserted now, except for the empty deckchairs. His bushy black eyebrows contrasted with his mane of white hair. Wrinkles around his dark eyes, slightly stooped shoulders. She had noticed that he wore several woollen sweaters on top of each other – his large, gnarled hands emerging from the sleeves as if they had lost their way – and socks that didn't match. And she remembers that she had smiled slightly at that. There had been long silences, with only the mountains as witness. She'd gazed at the treetops, wondering who would be first to break this fragile moment, whether she could find the right words or would stumble in mid-sentence. They had talked about the blue sky, their children, and the bitter lines around the stranger's mouth had softened. Then she had laughed at the idea of a frog in the shower. He had laughed as well and had said it felt good.

She gently pulls the curtains, lies on her bed and switches on the TV. *The Young and the Restless.* Can Sharon trust Avery?

She's shivering, and there's a funny feeling in the pit of her stomach. How about a hot bath? She looks under the letter 'D' in her address book and dials the number.

'Hello, Doctor.'

'Madame Delorme . . . are you back already?'

'I'm still in Bagnères-de-Bigorre. I feel all . . . feverish, yes, that's what it is, feverish.'

'Could be the start of a chill, perhaps. Or the change in temperature. Take two paracetamols, get a good night's sleep and you'll be fine in the morning. Come and see me when you return. I must leave you now: I have patients in the waiting room.'

'Two paracetamols . . . I don't know if that will be enough.'

14

Marcel is pacing up and down his room. How many years does he have left? He is older than his father was when he died. Now he's next in the firing line. Ten years? Fifteen? Fifteen years spent sitting on the bench and looking at Hector? Ever since the tragedy in Nice, he has had a constant feeling of being rootless. He isn't planning to be a museum piece, a useless widower. He looks at his hands as if they were detached from his body, as if they were his only way of expressing the best of himself.

He takes a black grape from the fruit basket, then a second, then the whole bunch.

The universe may shrink, but the heart doesn't. He misses carefree moments and laughter. He misses Nora's flowery dress. He misses Nora's forthright manner.

He remembers the night they camped in the rain, the torn tent, Nora's face laughing under the drips.

He remembers the light bouncing off the clustered white houses of Algiers, so bright it was almost blinding. And his uncle's café close to the port. They used to watch the old men playing interminable games of dominoes while chewing dried leaves and fig-wood cinders rolled in cigarette papers, with a glass of Ricard or of Beo beer never far away. They collected the cardboard beer mats and swapped them, then threw them up in the air and began again.

He has the taste of fresh, peppery mint on his lips, the taste of mandarins swollen by the sun, of hot harissa and the pistachio nuts they used to crack between their teeth. He has the din of the kasbah in his ears, all those languages intermingling, and the song of the goldfinch perched on the shoulder of a man walking in the Jardin d'Essai. The heady perfume of jasmine invades the room.

From Bab el Oued to Saint-Eugène, they had walked through the lively labyrinth of alleyways, past peddlers sitting on the pavement. One day they had boarded the tram without paying, and when the inspector wanted to check their tickets, they pretended to have lost them.

He remembers the tagines that Nora prepared under the affectionate supervision of her aunt. At the age of ten, she already knew all the ingredients: roasted almonds, soft prunes, raisins soaked in last night's water, cinnamon, lamb simmered gently in a terracotta pan. As delicious as their childhood. A dish filled with sugar and spice, tasting better each day, a dish to last you a lifetime.

The joys, the tragedies, he thinks, you never get over them. Images jostle for space, the best and the worst combined.

He remembers the frantic race back to the hotel in Nice. How often has he recalled that day? Each tiny detail branded on his memory. On the aluminium table in the morgue, a cold, rigid, blue body had replaced the little girl in shorts with her peachy complexion, her honeyed scent, her challenging eyes. An impossible goodbye.

He remembers her return to Vincennes long ago. She looked the same as before, but taller, more beautiful, more rounded. They had made love before they had even talked, with no preliminaries, their eyes wide open. He had entered her as if she were his home. Only then had he been tender, and they had exchanged their first kiss. He would like to be back in the hall on the evening of their ruby wedding, listening to the speech that she made. She has gone, for ever, yet he still gets up every morning; he is still breathing. Outliving her hasn't killed him.

Standing by the washbasin in the bathroom, he runs the cold water and splashes his face several times.

He looks out of the window. The empty deckchairs lie idle in the twilight. Why did he accept Manou's present? What is he doing here in Bagnères-de-Bigorre, locked up in this gilded cage? He'd have done better to choose the bison reserve at Lozère or the astronomy centre at the Pic du Midi. That meeting this evening on the terrace makes no sense. Nora was there, so very present. And yet that woman's grey eyes were full of sincerity. Upright, delicate, fragile, she made him think of a character in a novel. And then saying what she did about her loneliness. That had touched him.

He presses his thumb lightly against his right eyebrow, smooths it slowly twice, then does the same to the left. He imagines taking out the pins holding those white tresses in place, like the feathers of a bird with its wings bound. He opens the window to look at the empty terrace again. Scattered across the night, the lights of the villages sparkle like candles on a birthday cake.

Once again the wind has turned, and he doesn't know which way it's blowing.

15

Dinner is at seven thirty in the evening. She always sits near the columns, beside Paulette, who keeps regaling her with tales of her great-nephews. Which table will he have chosen?

She opens her wardrobe, looks at her dresses. Too pale, too dark, not cheerful enough. She is sorry she's never worn trousers. Trousers and a blouse would seem more youthful. Some powder, pink lipstick, a touch of eye-liner, a little mascara. When she was twenty, her lashes had been thick and curling. That was in another life. And a manicure can't do much for crumpled hands.

Should she go and sit at his table when he arrives or wait for dessert? He'll probably ask her to join him. She switches on the TV set again. Sharon and Avery are kissing. She switches the set off abruptly, drinks a glass of water, opens her book, closes it again.

She decides on smoky-grey stockings. Pulls a face as she puts them on. She hesitates between a necklace and ear-rings, pins her sister's brooch to the neck of her dress. She thinks of Louis Leduc's kiss in the playground at school, her cheeks blushing red, a hundred million light years away from the thought that one day she would be hiding the wrinkles round her neckline. A sugared kiss, a sweet that was unwrapped too quickly. She remembers that she whispered, 'I love you,' in his ear, because her best friend had told her that you did that whenever you kissed a boy. Her heart is beating fast, she feels warm, her head is spinning, so she sits on her bed once more, clad only in the smoky-grey stockings. Suppose she went downstairs dressed like that? She'd be on the front page of the local newspaper. She wishes she could leave ten years and a few wrinkles up here on the second floor, just for one evening. She thinks of Line Renaud singing at the Lido cabaret. Bagnères-de-Bigorre doesn't have a grand staircase like the one at the Lido, only a dining room. But every woman has the right to make a big entrance, with or without her feather boa.

But what if this is sheer nonsense? She walks slowly down the long corridor on the thick, peach-coloured carpet. She doesn't know whether she's doing it to gain some time or to compose herself a little. She looks all around the dining room. He isn't there. She walks on in like an automaton and sits down at her usual place. Paulette starts telling her about Benjamin, who has just begun to learn karate.

He's probably choosing which shirt to wear, the one with blue checks or the one with green stripes. It's seven forty-nine. At seven fifty-one he'll arrive.

On the menu: cauliflower soup, cod loin with creamed green beans, fruit salad. And water. Water again. If she dared, she'd order a vodka.

What if he's been taken ill? Someone ought to tell reception. She heard on the radio that smoking cannabis makes you feel brave. Paulette helps herself to more green beans.

'François has found a job in Luxembourg, as a legal adviser. It's an important position, and he's been promised he'll be promoted next year.'

Marguerite yearns for silence, so that she can remember the terrace, the creaking of the deckchair, the mane of white hair. He'll come in and he'll say he's pleased to see her again, he's been thinking about her, and he didn't dare to come down. The spa bath must have exhausted him; he's resting before dinner.

'And I haven't told you about my other sister's son yet, the one who lives in Argentina. He exports beef to English-speaking countries.'

Marguerite remembers what Frédéric had said: 'The mountains can't be agreeing with you.' He wasn't entirely wrong. She's let old, adolescent dreams surface again. All this dreaming about a worn-out old man. There's no sense in it. She gets up, leaving Paulette to her great-nephews. The magazines left lying around in waiting rooms have deceived her. When you're a widow, it's final. So go on – two paracetamols and then you go to bed.

She hopes the cold shower at eleven tomorrow morning will drive these silly ideas out of her head. For the rest of the day she'll avoid anywhere she might meet him. And then, from her room, she'll call reception, pretend to have a migraine and ask for some fennel tea with a slice of lemon to be sent to her room. She'll watch Sharon and Avery kissing on TV.

16

Marcel went to sleep on an empty stomach and has not had a good night. He woke up with the image of that character from a novel with the luminous grey eyes in his mind. He'll go down to breakfast, sit at her table and pick up the conversation where they left off.

She isn't in the dining room. She isn't at the buffet either. He stumbles on the step leading down to the veranda.

'That's women for you – they vanish into thin air,' he grumbles.

Deprived of coffee because of the house rules, he drinks a first cup of chicory, then a second. Just as he is spreading a thick layer of organic fig jam onto a slice of wholemeal bread, she passes by him without a word, her hair done up in a chignon that is more severe than ever. She goes to sit two tables away from him. There's an empty chair beside him. Why didn't she sit there?

Either she didn't see him or she's feigning indifference to attract his attention. He feels as if he's in a pensioners' playground. He recognises the sound of her voice.

'I'm not very hungry this morning, Paulette.'

Opposite her, a rather plump lady with short red hair is talking to anyone who cares to listen.

'I've brought some photos along. Look, the little one on the right is Benjamin, and then there's Camille, Jean-Charles, Adeline and François. The whole family on holiday at Cabourg. Delightful! And the oysters there – oh my word. I'm going back to the buffet. I could eat a horse.'

He can't stay put. The hell with convention! With a cup and saucer in one hand, sugar in the other, Marcel stands up and with a few steps he is sitting opposite the luminous grey eyes.

'Have you read the programme for today? Not so many activities planned. I feel like a rhinoceros that's halfway to freedom. Shall I take you out? Wear your trainers and bring your scarf – I'll see to everything else.'

Petrified in the moment, she hasn't put down the pot of jam that she was holding.

Paulette comes back and examines him with avid curiosity. She is holding a plate with a mushroom omelette almost drooping over the rim of it. Marcel hates the smell of eggs first thing in the morning.

'I'll meet you at five this afternoon, at the foot of the steps outside the hotel entrance. My car is a blue Peugeot.'

'Oh, I couldn't possibly accept.'

'What's stopping you?'

She stares at the label on the pot of jam.

'Do you get carsick?'

'No, but we hardly know each other.'

'We've talked about the sky and our children. Isn't that enough, madame?'

Paulette almost chokes on a mushroom.

'Oh, please don't call me "madame". My name is Maggy, or Marguerite, whichever you like.'

'I'll opt for Marguerite, but do please put down that pot of jam. It's not going to fly away!'

'I don't even know your name.'

'It's not the name of a flower, I'm afraid.'

'Do you know many men named after flowers?'

'Narcissus!' exclaims Paulette with satisfaction.

They politely agree with her.

'My name is Marcel, and now that the introductions have been made with all due form, will you accept my invitation?'

'Give me a moment.'

'I'll give you a moment while I go over to the buffet for a slice of rye bread.'

Standing by the toaster, he watches the two women

at the table. Marguerite is staring at the mountains in the distance. She gets up, settles her shawl around her shoulders, gives Paulette a slight nod, then climbs the few steps separating the dining room from the veranda.

'I wouldn't mind meeting someone at the foot of the steps at five. No, that wouldn't bother me at all,' suggests Paulette in a tenor's voice. 'How about it?'

17

After fifty-five years of a life where all the notes had been lined up as neatly as those on a Chopin score, she had been surprised to hear herself say, 'Why not?' She hadn't finished her breakfast, worried at having allowed confusion to interfere with the faultless journey to this point.

It is 5 p.m. Suede shoes, cotton trousers and, just as before, with several sweaters layered on top of each other, he is waiting for her beside a car unlike anything she has known before.

Henri never used to wear anything but impeccable grey flannel suits, with white poplin shirts neatly ironed by Maria.

Paulette is there too, on the third step, looking at the flowers in the large stone vase.

'I wouldn't mind coming with you if there's room.'

'I'm terribly sorry,' Marguerite stammers. 'I'm not

the driver. It's rather tricky, asking a gentleman I hardly know . . .'

'Personally I wouldn't entrust myself to a stranger. Do be careful – men can turn into werewolves.'

She leaves Paulette to her grim forebodings and joins Marcel.

'I'm pleased to see you . . . Lovely weather. We're in luck,' he mumbles.

'Not like last week,' she ventures.

'Give me a minute or two. There's a lot of stuff to organise in there.'

He mutters as he stows a backpack in the boot, and she likes this clumsy, ad hoc arrangement. Henri never surprised her. She feels a certain tenderness towards this man who is hesitant yet nevertheless has allowed himself to do something different.

'There, you can get in now.'

He holds the car door open, then closes it behind her. Before starting the engine, he looks at her for a moment, as if awaiting her blessing. 'Shall we go, then?'

The first fifteen minutes pass in silence. She feels as if they are adolescents, breaking the rules. What would Frédéric say if he saw her on a mountain road with a stranger, in a dented blue Peugeot? This man intrigues her, and her curiosity makes her panic. There's no point denying it – he's seduced her. With his layers of sweaters, his awkwardness and that fit of laughter on the terrace.

She sits up very straight, her bag clamped between her knees. He is there, concentrating on the road, so close to her, his large, gnarled hands on the wheel. She watches the muscles of his forearms tense as he changes gear. She leans back in her seat.

He chooses a CD. An accordion, a banjo and a mandolin merge with deep voices, invading the Peugeot.

'That's lovely,' she says.

'Chaâbi music makes you forget everything. It was part of my childhood, in the street, at the barber's, in the local café. Back there – everyone adores these tunes. Back there is where I come from: Algeria.'

A man from a mysterious country is taking her to a place known only to him, and she finds the thought intoxicating. She feels as if she were gorging on something deliciously sweet in secret.

After an endless series of sharp bends, he stops at a small parking space, opens the door for her and offers her his arm. She puts her hand on his wrist to steady herself. His skin is warm, covered in light, downy hairs; she falters, leans on his strong arm and allows herself to be led along the stony path.

At the end of the marked footpath, the view is breathtaking. A white sun, turning to scarlet, crowns the still mountains. Like ladies in broad-brimmed hats, the snow-covered peaks rise majestically towards the sky. In front of them, like a precious stone in its setting, is a sapphire-blue lake. Its clear surface reflects the sky and the fleeting clouds. And as if it were waiting for them, there is a large wooden bench facing the lake. A blackbird perched on a notice saying, *No bathing*, looks back at them. All is calm beneath the April sky.

No one has ever given her such a perfect moment before. Total harmony, the gentle air, the now comfortable silence between them. She did not know that such simple happiness could exist.

He takes a thermos flask out of his backpack, two cups, some dried apricots and some sponge fingers. 'I managed to get hold of some sweet things in the kitchen. Can I pour you a coffee?'

She drinks only tea, and after five in the afternoon it is usually herbal tea instead. If she says yes to this coffee, she won't sleep. But, in any case, all she'll want to do tonight is remember this experience.

'With two sugars, please.'

He rummages in his backpack. 'I'm an idiot! I forgot the sugar. Milk?'

'No, thank you.'

It's a lovely way to get to know each other, finding out how many sugars the other person takes in their coffee, if he or she prefers normal tea or herbal, strong coffee or decaffeinated, seaside or mountains, Saint-Malo or Bagnères-de-Bigorre. They talk about little things; one topic leads to another; the conversation is calm and becomes more natural.

'May I take a photo of you?' he asks.

She doesn't know why, but in this idyllic landscape it is nice to hear this man asking her that question.

'We're not supposed to be on holiday: we're here for the thermal baths.'

'Is that all?'

His mane of white hair, his tall body, his gnarled hands. She murmurs, 'Maybe not. I don't know.'

'I couldn't stand it the other day, with all those bits of cloth wrapped round me. I'd rather be out in the open air.'

'My husband and I used to visit the châteaux of the Loire.'

One day Henri's eyes had creased up and she thought that he was smiling.

'You look happy,' she had said.

'It's just the sun bothering me.' She never forgot that reply.

'I feel less closed in here. Do you know the Loire?'

'My wife and I belonged to a Scrabble club and we spent our holidays travelling all over France with its members . . .'

A cloud in the blue sky, thinks Marguerite. Paulette was right.

'Your wife doesn't like thermal baths?'

'No, it's not that.'

'I'm sorry.'

'She drowned in the sea at Nice, thirteen months ago.'

The blackbird swoops down beside the lake, puts out a claw, hesitates, then flies away.

'Life doesn't always turn out the way we imagined it,' she says gently.

'The most surprising thing is finding myself alone here with you, on this bench.'

The mountains stand in front of them in all their splendour, and a bell can be heard ringing in the distance.

'It's what people call a happy coincidence.'

'Destiny . . . *mektoub*, as we say in Algeria.'

'It's getting dark. Time to go back.'

They leave the landscape that has enveloped them with its benevolent presence in this singular moment. Again there is a silence that they don't recognise, a less comfortable silence. She doesn't want him to take her arm again; she would like to be somewhere else; all of this seems too intimate.

'I forgot to phone my son.'

'You can tell him you took an optional meditation session.'

'If I don't, I'll be asking for punishment.'

'The dunce's cap, do you think?'

They burst out laughing and the air seems lighter once again. The moon rises in the east, in a sky spangled with stars that is turning dark blue.

He whispers, '*Since night is destined for sleep, for unconsciousness and repose, for forgetting everything, why make it more charming than day, sweeter than dawn and dusk ... For whom is destined this sublime spectacle, this abundance of poetry cast from heaven to earth?*'*

'Do you like a starry sky so much?'

'I love Maupassant, and I haven't liked starry skies nearly so much since the accident. This is the first time I've rediscovered that pleasure. I feel as if Orion were watching over us.'

'Orion?'

'The constellation up there, always in the same place, north-east of Sirius and at an angle of forty-five degrees from Castor and Pollux.'

Sitting in the car, Marguerite can't help thinking that he, like her, lives alone.

* Guy de Maupassant, 'Moonlight'.

18

The suitcases are in the front hall. She is going to take the shuttle service to Tarbes Railway Station; he will be going home on his own. Paulette is handing out cards printed in old-fashioned typography, and assuring all and sundry that they'll be seeing each other again soon. Everyone agrees with her, without believing a word of it. His entire body knotted at the idea of saying goodbye to Marguerite, Marcel asks her, 'What will you be doing when you get back?'

'I'll make pancakes with my grandson. How about you?'

'I'm travelling on down as far as Collioure.' And in their private bubble amid the turmoil, he adds, 'Would you like to come with me?'

Marguerite, taken aback, removes a hairpin from her chignon, slowly puts it back, gathers up the skirts of her coat.

'I don't want to rush you into anything.'

'Could you lend me your phone?'

She takes a notebook out of her bag, searches for the number, then taps the keys brusquely.

'Hello, darling.'

'Is that you, Maman?'

'You've left the speakerphone on,' Marcel points out.

She turns to him. 'My son thinks the radio waves are bad for the brain.'

'Maman, where are you calling from?'

'I'm using a friend's mobile.'

'A friend's mobile?'

'I'll be back in a few days' time. He'll bring me home.'

'I don't understand.'

'I've already told you that you ought to consult a hearing specialist, but you never listen to your mother. I'm with a friend. He's taking me to Collioure for a few days.'

'Who is this friend you're talking about?'

'Don't worry – he's very nice.'

'And you're going off with him, alone? Are you sure this man is respectable? What kind of car does he drive?'

'A blue one.'

'What do you mean, a blue one? And what am I going to say to Ludovic? Don't forget that you're a grand-mother!'

'Yes, you're right, dear. I ought to be making jam and knitting a scarf for Christmas. Kiss my grandson for me and ask Maria if she can stay until Wednesday.'

'I'll see about Maria. And don't forget your seat belt.'

Marguerite smiles. She thought she detected his mind thinking, Chastity belt.

The son was definitely an awkward character. Manou had said only, 'You sound OK, Papa. Be good, take care of yourself, and don't forget to eat properly.' They left in haste. Paulette interrupted her lengthy farewells to watch them pensively. At least there was that piece about Jacques Cousteau on the radio to distract them.

Marcel does not give the receptionist at the hotel near the port a chance to ask any questions. 'We'd like two rooms, please.'

Marguerite looks from the potted plant on the counter to him; he mumbles, 'It's the sensible thing to do.'

They are soon down in the hotel lobby again, and like every couple arriving in an unknown place, they go in search of the tourist office. But they soon stop looking at the map that has set out a route for them, preferring to lose themselves in alleyways at their leisure, discovering picture galleries, havens of peace created by sculptors and the hidden cellars where potters display their ceramics.

They stop at a place that specialises in the preparation of anchovies, and admire the skill of the workers preparing the little fish.

'When I used to go on holiday, I'd usually bring back my son a framed reproduction of Azay-le-Rideau, a guide to Chenonceau or a medallion depicting Blois, but this time it'll be some jars of tapenade and anchovy fillets in vinegar.'

As she pays for her purchases, Marcel spots the photo of a serious old gentleman wearing a tie in Marguerite's wallet.

They end their walk near the lighthouse. As night falls, the hills are decked in red and ochre lights. Pretty as a postcard, or even better.

'I have an admission to make. This is the first time I've stood looking out at the sea with a man.'

Marcel takes off his glasses with a sudden movement, and there, on the pier, he decides to tell her everything about the Scrabble match and the tragedy on the beach at Nice.

Marguerite puts her hand on his. 'I'm so sorry. I didn't know.'

'No, it's me. We always put off the moment for talking about such things, but we ought not to.'

The small, wrinkled hand and the large, gnarled hand stay together for a moment.

The hotel proprietor has recommended a restaurant that specialises in Catalan dishes in the village. They move away from the sea which, for Marcel, is no bad thing.

'What would you like to eat?'

'I'm not even sure that I know what I like.'

There is a plate of sardines on the table next to theirs. Marcel remembers going fishing on the shores of the Mediterranean with a party from school and their biology teacher. As he was taking a fish off the hook, Nora had cried, 'Oh, how could you? Can't you see how he's struggling?' She had thrown all the fish he had caught back into the water. Marcel hadn't said anything, and on the way home he had taken her hand for the first time.

He orders grilled prawns, barbecued shellfish, shredded cod and a bottle of Banyuls. There must be something she'll like among all that.

He fills two glasses and raises his with a wide smile.

'Here's to the pleasures of being wrapped in green mud.'

Shyly, Marguerite responds by raising her own glass. With warmth coming to her cheeks, she replies softly, 'Here's to life and its pleasant surprises.'

She takes a piece of bread, puts it down, drinks a sip of wine and looks up at a black-and-white drawing of Collioure: elegant figures from the early twentieth century out walking, wearing straw boaters or holding umbrellas.

'I like that drawing behind you.'

Marcel turns to look at it.

'My marriage to Henri wasn't the kind that I dreamed of when I was a girl.'

As they leave the restaurant, Marguerite jumps nervously.

'What is it?'

'I've just seen a colleague of my husband's.'

Marcel stands up very straight, spreads his long arms wide and says, laughing, 'I'm your screen.'

'I know what he's like – if he sees me with you, it'll be all over Maisons-Laffitte in three days' time.'

Marcel is touched by the way she looks like a young girl caught in the act of doing something naughty. And then and there he kisses her for the first time. On a Tuesday in April, in Collioure on the Côte Vermeille of the Eastern Pyrenees.

Mouth to mouth, standing perfectly still, breathing in together, they sigh. A sigh of delivery and abandonment.

'Good evening, Madame Delorme.'

'Maître Damoiseau . . .'

'I didn't recognise you at first.'
She leaves that unanswered.
'Enjoy your holiday, madame. My regards to Frédéric.'

19

Those three days passed like a single day. Sitting on her velour sofa, Marguerite murmurs, 'I must have been dreaming.'

The ivory of the walls, the oriental carpet, Henri's empty armchair seem so far away from the deckchairs, the lake and Marcel's deep voice. He dropped her off at her door and simply said, 'Isn't it funny that we live so close to each other? I'd like to see you again.' Was that out of friendship or love? She doesn't know what to think. Suppose she phoned Dr Dubois? *I'm looking after myself ... Yes, the seaweed was lovely ... A man kissed me.* She closes her eyes to recapture the sensation of their hands touching, the delicacy of his kiss. Beneath his apparent resemblance to an old oak tree, she could sense a vulnerability that moves her.

'You don't turn down an opportunity.' Her father's words come back to her like a boomerang. If she'd boarded the shuttle for the railway station, she'd have been turning down that opportunity. He had taken two rooms. Looking at the green leaves of the rubber plant, she had felt both relief and a flicker of disappointment. It was all so different from the mannered world and its worthy citizens that had never really suited her in the first place. And so she had made her confession. The words had been there inside her for many years, but she'd never voiced them, except to this stranger who had held her hand below the blue-and-white checked table-cloth and hadn't let go. Life can sometimes be magical and fragile; that was something else she didn't know.

She remembers the first time Henri kissed her. It was during their honeymoon in Villandry. She'd been bored to death. Grand state rooms, toile de Jouy wallpaper and, as the highlight of their stay, a reconstruction of a jousting tournament, complete with knights in armour and coats of arms. Henri hated any lack of precision; their room was spacious, with a clear view of straight garden paths, rose bushes neatly lined up, honeysuckle well pruned and topiary trimmed into sculptured shapes. It was all perfect and predictable, like Henri himself.

He had smoothed the creases of his trousers before hanging them over a chair, and then he had put the light out. Under the white sheet, their lovemaking resembled love only in name; it was leagues away from the fantasies that Hélène had talked about on their visit to Rome. Leagues away from Emma Bovary *pulling at the thin lace of her corset, which would fall about her hips like a sliding serpent.* The chambermaid who brought their breakfast had tried exchanging a conspiratorial smile with the newly-weds. Henri had remained as impassive as marble. At the beginning of their marriage, he used to join her in her bed twice a month. Then once a month. Then not at all, as if he had forgotten to write, *Perform conjugal duties,* in his diary. He did the deed furtively, almost guiltily, ignoring her scent and the softness of her skin. He had never again looked at her as he had on that first evening; never again had they danced together. Even the lilac handkerchief in his breast pocket disappeared. Marguerite realised that she and he would never laugh heartily together at anything, and she had wondered whether another woman, in her place, would take a lover.

An envelope on the pedestal table catches her attention. It is addressed to her.

Madame Delorme,

When you find this letter, I will no longer be working for you. Your son told me to leave the house at once. I'm very upset. After thirty years of good, loyal service, I have to give you my notice. I have put the dresses back in the wardrobe. I've made some apple jellies. They're

on the shelf at the back of the kitchen. I'll think of
you when I'm listening to Chopin's second sonata next
Wednesday.

Your devoted Maria

Incredulous, she clutches the letter in her hand, reads it again, then puts it down on the pedestal table, opens her suitcase, takes out a bottle of Banyuls and a jar of anchovies, and says out loud, as if for the benefit of the entire building, 'How dare he?'

She pours herself a small glass of wine, drinks it straight off and is about to drink a second when the sound of the doorbell interrupts her.

It's him! He's going to take her to some far-off place to discover an unknown land, to meet lost tribes in the jungle. What a good thing she hasn't put her suitcase away yet. A glance at the mirror in the front hall and she opens the door, ready for anything.

'Papa dropped me off. He'll be here in five minutes.' Panting, red-cheeked, Ludovic hugs her, then runs into the sitting room, throws himself on the large sofa and, as usual, makes himself a little hut out of the cushions. 'He says the mountains have made you a bit silly.'

'What do you mean, silly?'

'He says you've been doing silly things, and you're too old for that.'

'Listen, Ludo dear, I'm going to tell you a secret.

You're always telling me about little Émilie who does gymnastics with you? Well, I've met a gentleman.'

'Doing gymnastics?'

'No, sitting in a deckchair.'

'Your eyes are all shiny.'

'Shall we make some doughnuts?'

But Ludovic isn't dropping the subject.

'Did you kiss him, like people do when they're in love?'

'And have you kissed Émilie?'

'I'm afraid she won't want me to. She once told me I was too fat when I couldn't manage to get up the rope ladder.'

'Don't worry, darling – you'll soon be able to climb to the top of the ladder and kiss Émilie in the playground.'

'You didn't tell me: do people still kiss when they're old?'

'Yes, they do.'

'And how about you? Are you really and truly old?'

The front door is closing.

'Ssh! Love stories are our secret.'

Ludovic winks at his grandmother, then buries himself under the cushions. Marguerite takes her son into the kitchen and asks him to sit down.

'I had a letter from Maria. What happened?'

'She was acting as if she owned this place. I've had the security camera put in, and even if it doesn't strike you as useful, it adds value to the house. They'll come and install the alarm next week.'

'This is my house, and I am still capable of making my own decisions.'

Frédéric is taken aback. 'I've never heard you talk like that before!'

'Then you'd better get used to it. Don't forget I'm seventy-eight years old.'

'Yes, that's the problem.' Frédéric's gaze moves to the table. 'Are you drinking wine, at five in the afternoon?'

'I've brought you some marinated anchovies, but I don't know if this is the right moment for giving presents.'

'Even Carole thinks it was insane, the way you left us without telling us what you were doing. When I think of all the things that could have happened to you. More and more senior citizens are going missing. Four a day. I read it in the newspaper.'

'Well, something did happen to me.'

'Your knees?'

'No, not my knees. Really, you don't understand at all! It's my heart.'

'Your heart?'

'It's racing.'

'Listen, if you're having palpitations, you should make an appointment with a cardiologist as soon as possible.'

'Do you know Collioure? It's a lovely place, and even more magical in the April sunlight . . .'

'The hell with Collioure. You must phone Dr Dubois and get him to give you the name of a good specialist.'

'I don't need a doctor. I need to dance in the rain like Gene Kelly.'

Leaning back against the sink, she thinks of the dear little boy who used to run into her arms when he came home from boarding school. What has become of him?

Frédéric wishes his father were still here to cope with this crazy situation. Were he alive, everything would continue as before.

'You've had a drink. And that man is bamboozling you. I'll bet he pretends he's just there at the spa to take the waters, when what he really wants to do is get his claws into some elderly lady. You wait and see, he'll end up stealing our silver. I forbid you to see the man again.'

'His name is Marcel, Marcel Guedj.'

'Guedj?'

Frédéric frowns. He's heard the name before, but he can't quite place it.

'And you're treating me like a child. I'm not fifteen.'

'Exactly.'

'It's my life, and I'll spend what's left of it as I want to. Sometimes I feel as if I've missed out on everything that really matters. I'll tell you something – this is the first time a man has given me so much joy.'

'You've lost your head.'

'No, my head's in the clouds, up among the stars.'

'That's just what I said.'

He leaves the kitchen, and a few minutes later she hears Ludovic crying. Then the front door closes again. She is alone with the wine that makes you confide in people. Well, so what if it was just a magical interlude, a delicious sweet that melted too quickly, a mirage? Three days in Collioure, destined to dissolve into thin air.

She met the man at the other end of France, but as it turns out, they live only a few kilometres apart. Fate? *Mektoub*, as they say where he comes from. She pours herself another glass of wine.

'To happy coincidences!'

Henri, posing in front of the Château d'Amboise, looks at her severely from the shelf where the boxes of tea stand. She leaves her suitcase at the front door, her glass of Banyuls half empty, Maria's letter on the table, and dials the number that he scribbled down on the packaging of the jar of anchovies. 'You have reached Marcel and Nora's apartment. I'm sorry, we're not in at the moment.'

She lets a brief silence pass, takes a deep breath and in a trembling voice says, 'I just wanted to say thank you.'

20

He knows exactly where to find the handbag that she took to Nice. He has given all her bags away except this one, and he has strictly forbidden his daughter to touch it. He always puts it back in the same place. On the third shelf, to the left, beside the red-and-blue swimsuit. His hand hovers over the bag for a moment, but when his resolve falters, as is the case today, he finds he can't resist the temptation. He opens the door of the wardrobe, delicately takes out the handbag, puts it on the table after holding it close, strokes the raffia with his large hands, gently opens the metal clasp with a click, removes the contents and spreads them out in front of him. Always in the same order. First the bottle of perfume. He resists the impulse to spray the last few drops on the inside of his wrist. Then the lipstick. He takes the top off it, draws a line the colour of rose-wood on his hand. On the diary page for 9 June is a dentist's appointment for 5 p.m. Missed because of a swim from which she never returned. A magazine full of unfinished crosswords. Seeing her sloping handwriting in the squares upsets him. In her purse, three fifty-cent coins, two twenty-cent coins and an old cinema ticket for a 9.30 p.m. screening. A photo, the colours faded; it shows her blowing out the eleven candles on her birthday cake, and he is beside her, clapping. He kisses the tube of lipstick and murmurs, 'Forgive me.'

He switches on the radio, in an attempt to get rid of the octopus squeezing his throat. Marguerite has reanimated something in him; a light is making its way into the darkness; his heart and body are coming back to life. He thinks of all those people who are living a new life. But this woman, met by chance, doesn't know anything about Algeria or his village. Nora knew every detail of their lives by heart. Theirs had been a childhood love affair, unique and irreplaceable. This faded photograph of a birthday cake. People should never grow old. He is overwhelmed by all they had in common; she left him too soon. And what if fate had tilted the other way and reversed their roles? What would she be doing now?

He puts on his overcoat, slams the front door behind him, descends the staircase and walks towards the square as fast as he can. He sits down at a table near the window at the back of the café there, watching the double-parked cars and the heads of drivers craning to spot their children. His watch tells him it is 4 p.m. There she is. It moves him to see her surrounded by her pupils. She greets the parents, buttons up a little girl's coat, kisses a colleague. Maybe the colleague is Françoise; he's often heard her talking about Françoise. She crosses the road, sees her father on the other side of the window and pushes open the door of the café.

'Hello, darling. Do you have time for a coffee?' he asks.

'Well, it's not every day I find my father waiting for me when I come out of school.'

'I always did.'

'Yes, but that was thirty-five years ago. You're not about to lift me up on your shoulders and give me a piggyback now.'

'You used to kick me to make me go faster.'

'A year ago I did need you . . . not to ride on your shoulders; I just wanted you to give me a hug.'

Manou takes off her jacket and puts her school bag on a chair, then sits down opposite her father and looks him in the eye.

'I give you a visit to a spa and then you go and vanish into thin air. I was afraid that something had happened to you. You're not a young man any more. I was worried.'

It always comes as a shock to Marcel. Her generous

curves, her black hair, that husky voice. Everything about her reminds him of Nora.

'Where have you been these last three days?'

'In Collioure.'

'But you haven't gone anywhere near the sea since . . .'

'It was different there.'

'You're lucky. Personally I can't go within fifty kilometres of the Mediterranean now. It's more than I can bear.'

'I didn't save her.'

'But you weren't on the beach, Papa.'

'I ought to have been with her instead of searching for a word that would win me fifty points.'

Manou sees the lines on his face, his hair, whiter than ever, the blue veins on the backs of her father's hands. He is on the verge of tipping over into the grief she knows only too well, but which she has never shared with anyone.

'It was an accident.'

'I wish I had died instead of her. You need your mother, and the worst of it is that I hate being the one who is left.'

Manou looks at the tall lime trees lining the road and whispers, 'I miss her too.'

So many silences between father and daughter. A few months ago, as she was giving dictation, she had dissolved into tears in the middle of a sentence and had abandoned her class. She had come back murmuring something to the effect that sometimes things were difficult. She hadn't dared tell her pupils the truth: that Nora's death had overwhelmed her so much that she was drowning. The next day she had found a drawing of a large red sun on her desk.

'Maman was lucky enough to leave when she was still beautiful and in good health. She didn't live to see herself grow old. We have to hold on to that thought.'

Marcel lowers his head. 'I never said goodbye to her.'

She has heard this phrase too often; it's always the same. The only thing he says. Manou stirs her empty cup with her spoon. A few weeks before the tragedy in Nice, she and Nora had organised a girls' night out together. Sake and secrets. Every time she passes La Maison de Tokyo now, she turns her head. She can't even say the word 'sushi'.

'Why did we all live through this sadness each in our separate corners? The first person I would have wanted to talk to about it was conspicuously absent; I felt as if I'd lost my father too.'

He murmurs, 'I'm sorry. I didn't know how to fight it. I was devastated too and I didn't want to make our grief even worse.'

'I know, Papa, I know. Forgive me. Wouldn't you like something to eat?' She smiles. 'Something nice and sweet?'

He loves his daughter so much. Not always in the way she wants, and sometimes he has an awkward way of showing it, but he does love her very much.

'Are you still single?'

Paul, the new French teacher, invited her to the cinema last Wednesday. After the film they walked for a long time in spite of the wind, and for a moment she enjoyed it very much. Her parents had married over fifty years ago, and nothing had diminished their happiness. She wants the same: if not, she'd rather have nothing.

'I've had some pleasant encounters, but that's about as far as it goes.'

'Yes, pleasant encounters . . .'

'With Maman, it was more than a pleasant encounter.'

Outside the school, the ballet performed by the cars is over. The headmistress comes out last, and Monsieur Mathot the caretaker locks the gate. There isn't a single pupil left on the pavement. She sometimes reproaches herself for not having given Nora the pleasure of being a grandmother. Her mother loved buying presents for her friends' many grandchildren when they were born.

Marcel is nervously breaking sugar lumps in half, without adding any to his coffee, and he taps the cup with his spoon to attract her attention.

'Anyone would think you were about to make a speech.'

'It's not a speech, but I do have something to tell you.'

Manou is surprised by his solemn, confident tone. She hasn't heard him talk like this in a year. The film stops on the image of father and daughter. People at the neighbouring tables are discussing what to have for dinner that evening, or ticking the boxes on lottery slips, hoping to change their lives and start again from zero.

He looks into her eyes.

'I wasn't on my own in Collioure. I met someone on the terrace in Bagnères-de-Bigorre. It was a happy coincidence, that's what she says.'

Manou nervously searches through her bag, finds a crumpled packet of cigarettes and goes out to smoke one on the pavement. Then a second. Is it the cold making her tremble?

A pane of glass separates father and daughter. The confession has stopped there. It was neither the time nor the place for him to tell her all about it. He puts the scattered sugar lumps back in their bowl.

Manou crushes her cigarette end under her heel and goes back into the café, puffing out the last of the smoke.

'Papa, don't tell me you've fallen in love with one of the young masseuses at the spa.'

'It's not like that. She's a woman of my own age. Her name is Marguerite.'

The race is about to begin on the large TV on the wall. The betting is to place the first five horses only. The horses, all mares, are about to cross the starting line at the Vincennes racecourse. The mares will race over two thousand five hundred metres, the preferred distance of the one called Belle de Mai.

He settles the bill, and they set off along the roads of Maisons-Laffitte. She slips her arm through his. The tears that have been frozen for the last thirteen months flow gently down Marcel's wrinkled cheeks.

When they arrive outside the apartment building, they spy a Pekinese with a big ribbon bow on its head – an exact copy of the bow its mistress is wearing – and they burst out laughing in the way they used to laugh when she was little, and they would sit on the balcony, watching life go by.

21

~~~

'My dear Hélène . . . it's a miracle! I'd never thought such a thing would happen to me. His name is Marcel, and I met him in Bagnères-de-Bigorre.'

She removes some faded flowers from the grave. She will come back and leave a bunch of daisies on Path S, Plot 17.

'If you only knew – he put his arms around me and kissed me. It was astonishing . . . He's from the south, he listens to music from a faraway place, and he's on first-name terms with the stars. I wonder what will come of all this. What will he think of my body – the body of an old woman that has been hibernating for so long? Do you think that after years of chastity, you turn back into a virgin? I don't know where I'm going, darling, but I will tell you one thing: I feel good.'

. . .

No visit to Henri and her father today. She meets the caretaker nearby. He is sweeping round the graves, careful not to leave any leaves lying around.

'Path L, Plot 32, you want to think about renewing your parents' lease. It runs out in December. After that you won't have to bother for another thirty years.'

He hasn't lifted his eyes towards her. In thirty years' time she'll be dead and buried herself. Life is for the here and now! She decides to take her chances at the hairdresser's without an appointment.

'You're in luck, Madame Delorme – we've just had a cancellation. A shampoo-and-set, the same as usual?'

She sees her reflection in the mirror. Who is that woman with the severe chignon?

'No, Hubert, let's have a change. Cut it short.'

'But, madame, your chignon is so much a part of you.'

'Exactly, and I don't want it any more.'

'Are you sure?'

She no longer cares about gossip and social niceties; something has taken over her. All the bubbles of mischief suppressed by Henri over the years are finally surfacing, ready to be set free.

She watches the locks of hair as they fall on her knees. Raising her head, she sees a nice symmetrical square.

'Go on, Hubert, carry on. Make it like Line Renaud's!'

· · ·

With her hair cut short, tousled like feathers in the wind, she feels lighter. She has left the old Marguerite in the salon and is putting up resistance to what little time she has left. On TV the previous week, she saw her favourite singer wearing a colourful trouser suit. She wants the same thing. She'll find it at Lili's in the main shopping street. As she leaves the shop, she exclaims, 'Maria! I'm so glad to see you.'

'Is that you, madame? I didn't recognise you.'

'I'm really sorry about what happened. I don't know what got into my son's head.'

'It was enormously hurtful, yes.'

'I wish you'd come back to the house.'

'I've enjoyed working for you, madame, but I've been thinking, and it's time I retired. I've been cleaning for thirty-five years, and my legs aren't up to it these days. I'm going to go back to live near my daughter in Portugal and enjoy the sun and my grandchildren.'

'Well, I'll miss you, but you're right, Maria — we have to turn our backs on our former lives. Shall we have lunch together? I'd like to say thank you for everything you've done for me.'

'Oh no, madame, that's not necessary.'

'But I'd enjoy it. I'm inviting you to La Grande Table for lunch next Wednesday. You can tell me about Portugal, and I'll tell you a secret of my own.'

22

They met eight hundred kilometres away from Maisons-Laffitte. He could have passed by her on the corner of Rue Jean-Mermoz and Rue de Lorraine, or in the marketplace. He wouldn't even have noticed her at the time. The only woman he saw was his wife.

Every Monday, like a ritual, he used to go and meet Nora for a drink at the end of her shift at the mini-market. They would tell each other about their day, and then they would go to the cinema. Today, for the first time, he has gone back to the Cosy. The waitress knows that Nora isn't simply away, but they won't mention the subject. You don't talk about the dead as if you were discussing the weather.

An old gentleman is sitting on his own at a corner table. His jacket is buttoned up the wrong way, his hair is untidy, and his eyes are dazed. He isn't turning the pages of the newspaper that sits in front of him. Only yesterday Marcel would have recognised himself in that man, bowed down by the weight of his grief. The impossible choice between dying and growing old. Their solitude shared, but not soothed. Passing from childhood to adulthood means losing your illusions one by one. From adult life to old age there are other things to be renounced. Sometimes the mind fails faster than the body. Sometimes it's the other way around.

A few months ago he'd had to give up playing dominoes with his friend Georges, who could no longer make out the number of dots on the tiles after his failed cataract operation. Since then Marcel has been leaving some of his shopping on the ground floor of the apartment building, so that it takes him several round trips to get it all up to the second floor. Beginning the day, loosening up his stiff joints, getting out of bed, washing, dressing, making breakfast, all of this takes time. You have to accept being less than you were; you must summon up the courage to fall into another rhythm. And now life has offered him this amazing present. Why him and not this other man? Does a new love story mean the betrayal of the old one? Did the manager of the reptile house who whispered her phone number to him twenty-five years ago trouble him for an instant? No. He never desired any other woman but Nora. He knew only the love of his youth. He'd been so lucky to meet her. It was *baraka*, an abundance of good fortune, as they say in Algeria. But now that is over. His old life has gone. Yet he still feels the need to give, to bury his nose in a woman's neck, to caress her; this desire is stronger than anything, even though his lined and weary body tells him something different. Taming this desire feels like climbing a mountain, but the idea of remaining alone seems insurmountable to him. All of a sudden time is running away from him too fast. How many grains of sand are there left in the hourglass?

He thinks again of the terrace at Bagnères-de-Bigorre. He had felt at ease there, but not to the point of telling her that he didn't like her chignon. He remembers his bold invitation at breakfast, and his clumsiness when she accepted it. He would have liked to have found the words to make her laugh at the start of their excursion, but he had just stood there beside his Peugeot, his arms dangling. Like a young man on his first date. Later, Maupassant had saved the day for him. His parents had once taken him to the coast of Normandy. He had been fascinated by the huge rock that was shaped like an elephant plunging its trunk into the sea. He had stuck a postcard of it in his diary, and back at school, his teacher had read him the passage about the little port of Étretat from *Une Vie*. Some encounters stay with you for the rest of your days.

. . .

How they had enjoyed Collioure! It was all so simple. There was something about Marguerite that he liked enormously; she had an aura of kindness, of innocence.

She had confided in him, he had opened up too, and they had talked freely. Maybe that was why they had kissed. It didn't matter. There was no need for him to understand the origin of his confusion.

Their first kiss. The second first kiss of his long life. So one could love twice? If he'd seen her sitting on a bench in the park, would he have asked if the space beside her was free?

He thinks of the long drive back. She had fallen asleep, snoring very softly. Maybe that was happiness?

His coffee is getting cold in front of him. The wrapper of the chocolate that came with it displays a picture of Venice.

And what if he took her there? A little hotel in an alley-way, far from the hurly-burly of the Piazza San Marco. He will keep this wrapper, put it in an envelope and write on the envelope, *How about the two of us go to Venice?*

The old gentleman is still sitting with his newspaper on the table in front of him. Marcel feels like wishing him a good day. He confines himself to a slight nod of the head. We confine ourselves to the minimum only too often.

He goes back to the main road and imagines himself and Marguerite in the city of the *doges*. He wants to do something new; it doesn't matter what. Immediately. He goes into a shop, buys a pair of leather moccasins and decides to keep them on. The soles are comfortable; he can walk more easily in them. He's never before bought such an expensive pair of shoes; he even lets the salesgirl tempt him into buying some shoe cream to keep the leather supple.

His body and his mind highly sensitised, a trivial, almost superfluous image moves him to tears. It is an advertisement for a brand of perfume with a father and son looking at each other on a yacht.

A clock strikes twelve noon. He could always cook himself something nice for lunch. Two chicken wings with new potatoes browned in shallot butter. But first he will leave a message on Manou's answerphone. 'May I drop by tomorrow? I'd like to borrow your *Guide to Venice.*'

23

There is a beautiful bunch of yellow daisies on the door-mat, together with a card: *Hector is expecting us at 2 p.m. I'll pick you up.*

This time she doesn't hesitate to phone him.

'Did you know that daisies are my favourite flowers? You've given me so much pleasure.'

'The pleasure is mine as well.'

'Who's Hector?'

'Someone very old and very wise.'

Their conversation is short; perhaps she should have kept him talking, asked if he had arrived home safely, if he had slept well and felt refreshed after the long drive. But she has to be ready by 2 p.m., and she wants it to be a real surprise when he picks her up for their first official date. Her new trouser suit, a turquoise sweater, and she runs a comb through her short hair. When she opens the door to him, he blinks and says in a slightly shaky voice, 'You look wonderful!'

'Really?'

'You're twenty years younger.'

'My hairdresser is a genius. Where are you taking me?'

'Follow the guide.'

When they arrive in the car park of Vincennes Zoo, Marguerite suppresses a grimace. She has never liked to see an animal behind bars, their gaze imploring. She comes here only once a year, for Ludovic's birthday.

In front of the toucans, Marcel explains that he and his colleagues used to divide the space up like the spokes of a giant wheel. The large mammals were his special area. Further on, there is a rhino.

'That's wise old Hector. Sit down there and you'll see how very slowly he moves about. I won't say he moves elegantly, but he's surprisingly agile for an animal that weighs three and a half tons.'

'Is it true what they say about the powder that can be made from their horns, that it's an aphrodisiac?'

'Unfortunately that's what people think. Mankind is crazy enough to destroy those natural masterpieces. This one is caged, but at least he'll be spared.'

'So every morning for forty years you got up to come here and feed this pachyderm.'

'It was a pleasure to see him every day, and over time we developed a special relationship. And to see the

137

wonder on the children's faces, and hear them exclaim with fright when they look at his huge jaws – I've never tired of that.'

'My father used to take us to the Bouglione Circus. There was a tiger in the menagerie. One day we looked into each other's eyes for more than five minutes. Me behind a barrier. The tiger behind his bars. I was only a little girl, but I couldn't help feeling that he was begging me to help him. Ever since then I feel a piercing sadness whenever I see animals deprived of their freedom.'

'I'm sorry.'

'Oh, don't be. I'm delighted to meet Hector.'

'The feeling is mutual. Why don't we go to the cafeteria for some refreshments?'

'But you must be tired of the sight of it. Would you like to come back to my house instead?'

She busies herself in the kitchen and returns with a tray containing some madeleines in a glass dish, two porcelain cups and a silver teapot. Marcel, standing in the middle of the sitting room, hesitates, as if wondering where to sit down.

'Darjeeling!' she announces, indicating the sofa to him with a graceful gesture.

At the same instant it occurs to her that Frédéric has a key and might turn up unexpectedly, but she decides to enjoy the moment all the same.

'My garden has often made me very happy,' she says, pouring him a cup of tea. 'Only this year the roses aren't flowering as well as they usually do.'

'You don't want to plant roses too far north; it makes it difficult for them to bloom.'

'I really must find someone to help me with the garden; it's too much for me to manage on my own. And my husband could never tell the difference between an azalea and a geranium.'

A clumsy movement and the madeleines fall on the oriental rug. Marcel apologises, picks them up and waits for a moment, not sure what to do. He doesn't quite like to put them back in the glass dish. Marguerite smiles at him.

'Don't worry – there's always been too much fuss about that kind of thing here.'

'It may not quite be Chambord, but almost!'

She opens wide the French window overlooking the terrace and invites Marcel to sit beside her.

'I think we feel more comfortable on benches . . . and anyway, I like sitting in my garden beside you, the way we sat looking at the snow-covered mountains.'

He places his thumb lightly on his eyebrow and smooths it very slowly twice, first the left, then the right. She is moved by this gesture; it arouses a new feeling in her.

'Why did you just do that?'

'Because you unsettle me. For the last few months I've been walking around town with my eyes fixed to the pavement, but today I feel myself coming back to life, thanks to you.'

Henri never said anything as beautiful as that to her. At best, he might say, 'You look good this morning, Maggy.'

Marcel puts his arm round Marguerite's shoulders and holds her close, looking out at the rose bushes that are planted too far north.

'Let's go in. You're cold, and we ought to do the washing-up.'

'Two cups and one teapot. You wash; I'll dry and put them away in the cupboards. We're a team now.'

She puts the lemon in the fridge to keep it cool.

'It seems silly to have such a huge fridge just for me.'

'It's the same at mine: the fridge is half empty.'

'Do you know the songs of Line Renaud?'

She hums: *You, my little madness, my little grain of fantasy* ...

He gets to his feet, takes her in his arms, and between the sink and the table where she has been eating alone for the last seven months, they dance to the old-fashioned words that Henri never let her sing.

You who overwhelm me, you who overturn, everything that was my life ...

'It's not Chaâbi music,' she says.

'But it's about joy too.'

Not so long ago she had to wait for Maria to come on Tuesdays and Thursdays to have some company, and now here she is, dancing with a man in her kitchen in the middle of the afternoon.

He gives her some more advice about her rose bushes too, and then he goes home. She heaves a sigh of relief. Frédéric hadn't turned up unexpectedly.

It's 10 p.m. when the phone rings.

'It's me. I've been thinking about your garden; this is the time to plant daffodil bulbs. I know a very good garden centre and they don't put their flowers in cages there. We could go and get some bulbs tomorrow?'

She thinks of how to address this man, but somehow even using his first name suddenly seems too intimate, even though they have already kissed. So she simply says, 'I can't make it tomorrow. I have my grandson the whole afternoon.'

'Well, that would be a nice way for me to meet him, among all the daffodils?'

'Are you sure I won't just be doing another silly thing?'

'How old are you, Marguerite?'

She laughs. 'The right age to do silly things.'

'I'll come and pick you both up at 3 p.m.'

'We'll be ready. You'll recognise me easily – I'll be holding my grandson's hand.'

She takes her diary out of the desk drawer, and on tomorrow's page she writes, in capital letters, *3 P.M. MARCEL!*

A pretty country road leads to the Nettles Garden Centre. Ludovic talks about his tennis lesson, and Marcel tells him about the gilded cup he won in a basketball tournament when he was fifteen. Marguerite would like the moment to last for ever.

As they go up the long driveway that leads to the garden centre itself, Marcel invites Ludovic to sit on his knees and take the wheel. Neither his father nor his grandfather would ever have suggested such an adventure to him. With his hands at ten to two on the wheel, like a captain steering his ship into port, Ludovic is in charge. There is shouting and laughter all the way to the car park, where Marcel takes the controls again.

Ludovic turns to his grandmother. 'Papa says you're going to move house. Is that true?'

24

'Papa, can you come round right away?'

'Is there a problem?'

'I've just got back from school. I haven't even taken off my coat. We must talk at once.'

Marcel hurried round, climbing the stairs in haste. She didn't kiss him. He sat down on the velour armchair, out of breath.

'Ludovic . . . does that name mean anything to you?'

'Yes, he's Marguerite's grandson. Why?'

'He's in my class.'

'Is that so terrible?'

'There's nothing terrible about it, but Ludovic has a papa too.'

'Have you seen him?'

'I most certainly have.'

'What did he want?'

'He asked me if I knew that my father was sleeping with his mother.'

Marcel sits back in the armchair.

'He turned up in my classroom. He reminded me of an old umbrella rolled up too tightly, with his dark suit, his perfectly knotted tie and his shoes without a speck of dust on them. I'm used to seeing anxious parents, but this one took the biscuit. He was biting his lips so hard that his mouth almost disappeared. And there was I, with twenty-five pieces of geography homework to correct. He said you were my responsibility. Maybe you abducted your Marguerite in too much of a hurry.'

'We did tell you.'

'Yes, maybe you did, but it's also true that there are reasons for us to be worried.'

'I'm not a child.'

'You go off to Collioure. Three days after getting back, you pick up that woman and her grandson in your car, and to cap everything, you let him take the wheel.'

'You don't have a drop of cognac, do you?'

He hears the doors of the kitchen cupboards opening and closing; he hears the kettle whistling. He isn't going to get his cognac. He is surrounded by the furniture from their first apartment, a desk that Nora bought in a junk shop, schoolbooks on the table, on the floor, everywhere. A poster for a concert on the wall and a stack of DVDs beside the TV. A pile of love stories.

144

Manou comes back with the engraved silver tray. The tea ceremony, just as Nora used to serve it: plenty of mint leaves, two drops of orange-flower water, too much sugar. The same concentration as she pours the tea from a great height, the same satisfaction at having aimed it right into the glasses, the same expression when she picks up hers, which is still too hot.

'What did you say?'

'I asked him whether his mother was a minor and he didn't like that one bit. He's quite capable of complaining to the schools inspectorate. Guess what he said next? "This is no joke, mademoiselle. She's lost without her husband. Until my father's death we never had any problems in our family at all, and now she goes running off from a spa with a total stranger, and that stranger is your father. He took my mother to Collioure without my consent. She has to stick to a diet without any salt, she drinks only mineral water, and now I find her sitting at her table at five in the afternoon, in front of a jar of anchovies, and with a half-empty bottle of Banyuls in front of her. She has changed beyond all recognition, mademoiselle."'

Marcel ought to feel guilty, like a little boy caught being naughty, but the situation seems so grotesque to him that he simply wants to laugh.

'And what about you, Manou?'

'What do you mean, what about me?'

'What do you think about all this, darling?'

'I'd already spotted him at a parents' evening. He seemed so uptight. I'm sick and tired of parents who have insane dreams about their children's future. As if being a notary were the only profession for a notary's son. If I had children . . .'

The tea is boiling hot but delicious, as they both like it.

'No, I meant what do you think about me meeting Marguerite?'

She blows slightly on her glass.

'Well, it was rather a successful present after all. And to think that you almost ran for the hills just because you don't like asparagus soup!'

'Are you one of those women who believe that you only ever fall in love once?'

'At your age, I'd say every minute is worth ten years.'

She drinks some tea and looks into his eyes.

'I'm one of those women who thinks it will be fine tomorrow even if the weather forecast says it will be horrible. And in particular I'm one of those women who think they have a wonderful father. Now I must be off. I have to go back to school: I forgot to feed Jojo.'

'Jojo?'

'The class hamster. He needs me.'

'I need you too.'

'Would you like to come to lunch on Wednesday?'

146

25

Electric light bulb in her hand, standing on a kitchen chair, her right foot slips and Marguerite comes to her senses lying on the tiled floor, her heart thumping, the bulb smashed to smithereens. After hearing so often that she must be careful or she'll have a fall someday, it has actually happened. She tries to stand up. She pulls a face, pushes herself up from the floor and is on her feet. Her legs are working, and she's survived the fall fairly well. She hesitates between paracetamol and calling Dr Dubois. She opts for the doctor.

'Thank you for coming so quickly.'

'I happened to be close by.'

He reassures her: she will have some bruising, and her wrist is sprained, but she doesn't need a plaster cast, only a bandage. He takes her blood pressure and looks at her affectionately. With her short hair, she almost looks like a young girl.

'You live dangerously.'

'If you only knew, Doctor.'

'Well, you've had a shock. You should rest now.'

'I feel that my heart is beating rather fast.'

'I'll give you a tranquilliser.' He puts his stethoscope away in his leather bag and adds, 'I'd like a glass of water, but stay where you are. I'll fetch it myself.'

He comes back, holding the glass.

'Are you really all right?'

'Yes.'

'Well, it's not to be taken for granted, when you're living all on your own in this big house.'

'Especially since Maria left.'

'Luckily you have your grandson.'

'Luckily I've met someone.'

Dr Dubois straightens his shirt collar.

'Well, that's good news. Worth all the tonics in the world.' He smiles at her. 'But watch out for wobbly chairs.'

She wants to hear Marcel's voice. She settles down comfortably on the sofa, her arm resting on a cushion, and tells him about Dr Dubois' visit.

'For future reference, do bear in mind that I can plant daffodils *and* change light bulbs.'

'Can you make a béchamel sauce too?'

'It's one of my specialities.'

'I somehow can't get into the habit of using your first name.'

'It'll happen when you least expect it, Marguerite.'

How long has it been since she last laughed over the phone with a man? Well, to be honest, it has never happened before.

'I must go: I can hear footsteps. It'll be my son. He's coming to fetch some papers for the valuation of a picture.'

Frédéric has had a key ever since Henri's death. She's never liked the fact, but he insisted on it. When he comes in, the only thing he sees is the white bandage on his mother's wrist.

'It's nothing serious. I was simply trying to change a light bulb.'

'I've already told you not to climb on chairs. Ever since you went off with that stranger, you've been doing all sorts of stupid things. Cavorting about isn't right at your age.'

She tells herself that her son might try doing the splits from time to time himself; it's good for the soul. Carole can't be having a very amusing time of it either. A small, nervous laugh escapes her.

'Maman, how long has it been since you last went to the cemetery?'

'I don't see the connection.'

'Monsieur Buisseret, who worked for Papa, told me

that the grave isn't being properly tended. He was very surprised not to see a single flower on the granite slab.'

She nestles into the cushions like a naughty child taking her punishment. Her son bites his lower lip. He will come back later when he has calmed down, he tells himself.

At two in the afternoon he is outside the door once more, his hand on the handle. He knows he is about to do something difficult. He goes back to the road; he needs to walk. He hesitates and then dismisses all the doubts that might nibble away at his decision. He goes into the house and tells her, in a very calm voice, that he has found her a bed in a clinic. He adds that it's difficult to find a place where medical check-ups can be organised in a hurry. Marguerite doesn't understand at first; then she tells herself that if she'd had a cat, the cat would be a good excuse for her to stay at home. But it seems that things are more serious.

'You must rest. It won't be like Bagnères-de-Bigorre, but it is a first-rate establishment and was recommended by a friend of Carole's. There are good doctors there; they can tell if everything is all right.'

And who is going to water the flowers if she isn't here?

'You'll see, it's a very pleasant place, surrounded by trees, with attentive staff who can take good care of you. You'll feel better the moment you're through the door.'

She clutches a cushion more and more tightly.

'Don't you have anything to say? It's for your own good, Maman. You can't stay here on your own. Falling over like that was a wake-up call, and I do think you've been very confused recently. When we get the medical results, we'll decide what's best for you.'

She thinks of Marcel's forearms on the wheel of the Peugeot.

'You never did anything without Papa, and this is what he would have wanted. He always said prevention is better than cure.'

She thinks of the light on the hills of Collioure.

'Ludovic can come and see you on Wednesday.'

She thinks of Marcel's dark eyes on her all through dinner.

'You can come back here when you're well enough. I'll take you there, so put a few things in a bag and I'll bring you the rest later.'

Marguerite follows her son to his car, her mind clouded by Dr Dubois's tranquilliser. He takes a pretty road through fields of alluvium. The way into Beaulieu House looks like the entrance to a charming hotel, but once inside, she sees wheelchairs in the corridors, the distraught eyes of residents clinging to nurses, their weary bodies. A strong smell fills her nostrils, as if disinfectant had to be applied several times a day to fight off the scent of old age. She wants to go back to her own home, to sit on the bench in her garden and wait for the daffodils to bloom.

She walks behind him in silence. She hears his voice through a fog that reminds her of the way she felt at Henri's funeral. Her room overlooks extensive parkland.

'Look, poplars. You've always liked poplars.'

'Frédéric, where am I?'

'In a clinic. Full of healthcare professionals.'

'You're lying to me. All the patients here are old.'

'Please don't be childish, Maman. The staff here will look after you.'

He kisses her on the forehead and goes away. As he leaves, he passes the reception desk. He says, 'As we agreed, my mother will remain here for three days. After the tests have been carried out, we'll see if it's necessary to prolong her stay.'

Back in his car in the car park, he sits motionless, his hands on the steering wheel. Will the poplars be enough to reassure her? He would have liked to give her a hug, but somehow it didn't happen.

He remembers coming back from boarding school on Friday evenings in winter. She used to make him French toast, whirling around the kitchen in her dress with blue and white spots; today she has fallen off a chair because she's no longer able to change a light bulb.

Of course he has considered taking her home with him and putting her in the guest room. When he thought about seeing his mother at dinner every evening now that he is fifty, he rejected the idea. He has also thought about getting a carer for her at home, but there has been too much extravagance recently for her to be left alone there, even under strict supervision.

He knows that his father would have approved of the choice he has made. He dials the number of a client; he would like to arrange a meeting for tomorrow, to discuss that property deed and to forget the smallest fragment of emotion.

Sitting on the edge of the bed, Marguerite is alone, away from all her points of reference, as she was at the beginning of her marriage. She had left her parents' house of mourning for the austerity of her husband's house. From the mausoleum to the museum. It had taken her months to get her bearings. Where and when had she failed? The idea of boarding school had been Henri's, and she had gone along with what he said, as she always did. At the weekends he used to talk to his son about Chopin sonatas while she sat in the shadows, insignificant.

. . .

Frédéric has dumped her here the way some people might leave a cat by the side of the motorway before going on holiday. White walls. The room is empty except for a table, a chair and a bed. She has been found guilty of being seventy-eight years old. She's been sentenced to imprisonment for life. A storm is growling, and a flash of lightning streaks the pale wall with blue. Pain shoots through her wrist; the effect of the tranquilliser has worn off. She wants to see Ludovic and hold him in her arms.

A nurse comes in, carrying a meal on a tray.

'Aren't you in your nightie yet? Eat up, madame, and I'll come back and help you go to bed. You must rest — the examinations will begin tomorrow.'

It is six in the evening. She opens the plastic-covered containers and finds the slice of ham, the poorly braised chicory, the plain yoghurt: the kind of menu that is appropriate to her new life. Frédéric has closed the dossier. Stamped it with a neat little blow. Sorted and filed.

She looks at the poplars, the sky where the storm is breaking, her bandaged wrist, her bag. In the sudden departure, she forgot to bring the packaging from the jar of anchovies on which Marcel had scribbled his phone number.

26

He had come here when he first got back from Nice. This evening, after two days without any news, he hopes to regain his peace of mind by coming here again. He sits on the bench, facing Hector, in front of the bulk of imperturbable flesh. The rhino walks about with his heavy tread and then stops on the muddy ground. In the middle of his large head, his tiny eyes search Marcel's gaze.

'You haven't seen Marguerite, have you?'

The animal's immobility has always fascinated him. What if she doesn't want to have anything more to do with him? What if she has made some other choice? He gets to his feet and leans on the fence that surrounds the enclosure.

'I'll be back.'

Evening is coming on; he retrieves his car, goes back to Maisons-Laffitte, drives round the town at random, changes direction and parks in the road with the elegant homes. He rings the doorbell of number 25 several times. No reply. He walks around the house, looks in at a window. Although there is a crescent moon in the sky, he can make out nothing but shadows in the large sitting room. He sees the bench on which they confided to each other in the garden. He sits on it, his throat dry, imagining the worst.

Suppose she has fallen downstairs?

Suppose her heart couldn't stand up to all the excitement?

He hears a voice in the twilight. 'Can I help you?'

'I'm a friend of Marguerite . . . Maggy . . . Madame Delorme.'

'She isn't here. I saw her leave with her son yesterday. She had a bag with her.'

'A bag, as if she was going away for a long time?'

'I have no idea, monsieur! I am sorry to say that we don't much like to see strangers trespassing in the gardens here.'

'I'm not a stranger. I went to the seaside with her very recently.'

'There must be some mistake. Madame Delorme is a widow.'

'Don't worry, we took separate rooms.'

'Monsieur, that is none of my business. If you don't leave at once, I shall call my husband. And mind those begonias. I planted them myself, and Maggy is very fond of them.'

'Thank you for your kindness.'

If the tightly furled umbrella has taken her away, he'll have confiscated the phone.

He gets back into his car. It makes for the cemetery of its own accord. Always the same desire to talk to Nora when there's something on his mind. He stops at the gate and then decides against going in. A cold stone, a name, two dates. She isn't there.

He sets off again, muttering: why did she leave? What exactly did she say to me the last time we talked? She doesn't like to see animals in cages, and I went and took her to the zoo. He passes the chapel at the entrance to the cul-de-sac. Maybe I was going too fast. Maybe she wasn't ready for it yet. There's the local waste tip on the left. Manou is always telling me to sort out my things. Red light. Too late! He'd told her he thought of her each time he drank a glass of water. What an idiot! When you've only known a woman for three days, do you suggest taking her to Collioure? He said her rose bushes were planted too far to the north instead of offering to help her. He turns on the fog lights. He knocked the madeleines over onto her rug. There are fewer and fewer houses now; the street lighting is sporadic. She must have thought he looked out of place amid the glamorous surroundings of her home. There are only cows now, lowing in the night. He remembers her saying that her son had arrived, probably as a way of cutting the conversation short. He lowers the window and the wind blows in his face. She let the altitude intoxicate her, but once she was home again, she took control of herself. Very fast. Too fast. His headlights illuminate a small animal; he turns the wheel; the car swerves. A piercing squeal, a squashing sound. He has run over the hedgehog. A flattened, bloodstained ball lies in the road, beyond the help of even the best of vets. He picks up a branch and pushes it gently to the verge, where he leaves it among the stinging nettles.

I shall do something stupid if I go on driving like this. He takes the first muddy track on the right and turns off the engine. He doesn't want to look at the red mark on his tyre. He opens the boot, takes out an old rug and walks. A winding path, a meadow, a small wood; he goes on in spite of his tiredness and his aching ankles. He knows every blade of grass here, the hawthorn hedge, the tall ferns, the dry-stone wall. There is only one place where he wants to be at this precise moment, over there in the large clearing. He spreads his rug on the damp grass and lies down, crossing his arms. The vault of the sky, *this abundance of poetry cast from heaven to earth*, calm.

There are his stars. When he is in tune with them, he is in tune with himself.

Where are you, Marguerite? I'd do anything to see you again.

27

Beaulieu House

Dear Marcel,

I'm writing to you on a pale little table overlooking a park. I owe you the truth. My son brought me to this establishment for some medical tests. Over these last few days I've realised that it is also a retirement home for the elderly, and it will be good for my health, maybe even save my life. I never wanted to countenance such a thing, but now that I'm here, I keep telling myself that this place might be a solution. A more comfortable room will be available soon.

I have to be realistic; I know I'm tired. I thought I felt rejuvenated, but I'm seventy-eight after all, and I'm no Jane Fonda! Frédéric can get on my nerves, but I know he wants the best for me, and I don't want to cause him any anxiety.

Financially it's not a problem — that's the last

privilege of being a notary's wife. On the material level I've been spoiled; I was lucky enough to live in a nice house, and I'm still in the area I've always known. I am going to bring my bronze clock and some of my favourite paintings here, so that I'm not entirely starting again from scratch.

Maybe this will be your solution too someday.

We have to choose where we will spend our last years in good time. Later on we won't have the strength to do it because such major changes are too tiring. Today I tell myself I can't afford to be wrong.

Dr Dubois is getting old and will soon retire. Changing doctor, at my age, would be a great worry.

The other night, when I couldn't sleep, I worked out the number of times I've been up and down the twenty-three steps of the staircase in the last year. Four times a day for three hundred and sixty-five days. The idea of not having to do that climb is a relief. The house is too big for me, Maria is no longer there, and when I sit by the large bay window in the evening, I feel frightened.

The trip to Collioure was a wonderful break and it left a deep impression on me. I don't regret anything about it; believe me, I'm very happy to have had that experience.

I remember the little bench where we sat watching people playing bowls, and I remember the Dutch tourist wearing bright orange shorts who thought himself the local champion. I read somewhere that recollecting happiness brings more happiness.

Sometimes I tell myself that I ought not to have kissed you, or even to have let you kiss me. But a moment's abandonment is excusable, and maybe it was the south-westerly wind that turned my head.

I did toy with the idea of becoming a different person, but now I'm sure it isn't the time for me to play at being a girl again. We all get our turn at that, and mine was over long ago. But anyway, it was nice to take a little step off the beaten track.

I wonder how much time I have left. Three years? Five years? I'll spend them here in peace and quiet. I'm older than you. What if I fall ill in a year's time? I fell off that chair — it was a warning sign. What if I hadn't managed to get up? I could have been lying there for days before anyone found me. Sometimes we have to accept radical changes. It's a choice that I'm deliberately making. I need security, and I know that I have nothing to fear between these walls, which are not mine, but I expect I shall get used to them.

One Sunday, if you feel like it, you could come to see me. We'll walk in the park and I'll show you the poplars.

Yours sincerely,
Marguerite Delorme

28

Hello,

I've just read your letter and I feel as if Hector has sat down on my chest. I've been looking for you everywhere, I imagined something terrible had happened, and I made a promise to my stars: I promised them I'd find you. And today you're telling me that you're in prison and you want to stay there? I'm going to reply to you all the same. It's about a hundred and fifty years since I wrote a proper letter, and the last one was to the taxman when he got his figures wrong. You're wrong too. Not being able to change a light bulb doesn't mean you have to change your whole life. Stop counting the steps on your staircase and think what good exercise it is. Think of it as healthy. There'll be plenty of time for you to have a stairlift put in if you need one.

You mention that Dutchman wearing his orange shorts in Collioure as if it were your only memory of

the place; I have a thousand. Remember the strange
rice-milk ice cream we shared down by the harbour?
And the sudden shower when we came out of the
museum? What do you make of all that? You talk about
a step off the beaten track — as far as I'm concerned,
I could spend the rest of my life dancing with you in
your kitchen. I may be retired, but there are no wrinkles
on my heart. I don't want to go round the park at
Beaulieu House with you; I want us to go round the
world in a balloon. A place in a rest home? It would
never occur to me to shut myself up in a cage, and I can
rest at home on my divan perfectly well. It's your choice
to let yourself be manipulated by your son, Frédéric.
I can't conceive of our relationship being from two
to four in the afternoon, still less think of you sitting
there eating mush without any salt, when I can make
you a splendid couscous royale made with hand-rolled
barley. I can already picture you having dinner with
people like Paulette, and invalids lining up the pills
and capsules they need to take. Don't count on me for
Sunday visits. At your age not all women are equal —
you're a young girl of seventy-eight, and I could have
looked after you better than a bunch of anonymous
nurses. But you've decided on your own that it's all
over between us. After reading your sensible letter, I've
decided to go back to Algeria as soon as I can and find
myself some roots to cling to. Manou will understand.

She'll go there herself someday, and then I'll be able to show her the hills of our childhood and the house where her mother lived.

You suggest the south-westerly wind accounts for our kiss; there wasn't a breath of wind that day. There are some breaks from routine that one would like to go on for ever, and ours was one of them.

Marcel

P.S. I don't care for poplars. Too melancholy for my liking.

29

'A letter for you, Madame Delorme.'

A nursing assistant brings her Marcel's letter just before the afternoon's entertainment in the common room begins. Her hand shakes as she slips the envelope into the pocket of her long cardigan. This isn't the right moment to read it. Not right now. She'll read it later.

A man is standing in front of the rows of chairs. Beside him, a brightly coloured puppet covered in well-worn fur is singing familiar songs. Some of the residents join in the chorus. Marguerite's neighbour coughs a little too loudly.

'They really do treat us like children. I never liked going to the circus, or watching magic tricks, and I like ventriloquists even less. Why do they put us through this?'

'You could always stay in your room,' suggests Marguerite.

'I'm bored to death in my room.'

'Have you been here long?'

Marguerite is surprised to find herself entering into conversation so easily, experiencing this moment as if it were the most normal thing in the world. She knows the letter is there. She wonders why she doesn't just open it, as she would any other letter. Why is she making all this fuss? She isn't going to change her mind.

'I don't remember exactly when I arrived, but I've calmed down over the years. And about time too, at my age,' replies her neighbour.

'So you do get used to living here?'

'You're not really listening. Do you have hearing problems? Let me tell you, I'm deeply depressed, and my arthritis doesn't do much to improve matters.'

The old woman looks out of the window.

'I can feel that the wind is getting up and that will make the poplars dance. I like their gentle movement; it makes our destiny more bearable. At the age of eighty-two you take whatever distractions you can find. Are you amused by that grotesque puppet? My own story begins with a tragedy. Would you like me to tell you about it? Let's sit on the veranda; it will be quieter there, and closer to the trees.'

Marguerite hands the old woman her stick, adjusts the cardigan that has slipped off her arm and helps her to get up. She has never before listened to the confidences of a stranger.

In the distance, the brightly coloured ventriloquist's doll can be heard singing a song by Charles Trenet.

'I was only a child when the war devastated Dunkirk. Yes, I'm from the north; perhaps that's why I like it when the wind blows from that direction. The bombing had been terrible that week, much closer than usual. Our building had stood up to it until that Saturday evening in December. Was it a miracle or simply chance? On the nights when I can't sleep, I still hear my father's voice shouting, "Run, both of you! I'll meet you at the town hall."'

The two women watch the poplars swaying in the wind. The nurses come and go, getting their work done somehow or other. In her pocket, the letter burns Marguerite's fingers. She hopes he has understood and everything will be back to normal again.

'I took the blanket that I'd thrown round myself to muffle my ears, and I raced down the stairs four at a time, calling to my mother as loud as I could. I found myself on the pavement, wearing a nightdress. "Run!" my father shouted from our third-floor window. "We're coming." I hadn't even turned the corner of the street when my building collapsed, taking my life with it. A shell had eviscerated them both. Only a gaping hole in the ground was left, and all around it lay piles of stones, floorboards and window frames. I didn't shed any tears. I didn't scream. My only sensation was that of being submerged in a sea of ice. The tragedy has become more distant, don't ask me how, but I never go out without taking two cardigans with me, and some spare socks, whether it be summer or winter. So many years have passed since then. How time flies, doesn't it? Only a little while here and then it's all over. There are some good things in the middle of it all and you have to seize those opportunities, because if you don't . . .'

'Did you want to go back and look for your parents?'

'I never had the time to ask myself that. A woman took me by the arm and dragged me off to the town hall. The air raid was still going on, so she held me tight. I struggled, shouting that she wasn't my mother – my real mother was with my papa under the rubble of our building in the Rue des Fraiseurs, and all my dolls were waiting for me there.

'After that everything seemed to happen without it really affecting me. I went from foster families to hostels, from budding love stories that came to nothing to false dreams, without ever getting too fond of anything or anyone. And so here I am today, spending my time in the common room of an old folks' home, watching a ridiculous puppet show.'

Her forearms resting on the arms of the chair, her eyes fixed on the park, Marguerite lets a short silence pass, then asks gently, 'Were you ever married?'

'Almost. I once loved someone very much, but I missed my step and took a nasty fall. I'll leave it at that; the rest of the story is my own and it's getting late. I haven't talked to anyone like this in a long while. What's your name?'

'Marguerite. What's yours?'

'Antoinette, but I've always been called Nénette.'

Dinner is about to be served. Nénette gets up, leaning on her stick.

'My first home collapsed before my own eyes, burying my parents. Can anything worse happen to you after that? And I know that this place, Beaulieu House, will be the last stage of my journey.'

She walks away slowly, glancing back at the park one more time before going into the dining room. 'It's beginning to rain,' she says as she leaves.

Marguerite is alone on the veranda. The ventriloquist has finished his act. She is aware of the emptiness of her life, of the absence of any close female friend. There had been her sister, but a patch of black ice on a road had changed the course of that story nearly sixty years ago. Why does she remain bound by her past like a dog attached to its lead? No close female friend, no one to love. Not the slightest risk of losing someone dear to her for the second time. She'd never had the strength to break out of the cocoon that Henri had so carefully woven for her. A cousin who lived on the other side of the country had inherited a little money when her mother died, and within twenty-four hours she had left the husband to whom she had seemed so devoted for so many years. That had always impressed Marguerite. It had all been so simple with Marcel. Simple but also complicated, like a game of seduction when she didn't know the rules. Her entire life could be summed up by saying she didn't dare. She had never dared. That sudden insight, as she looked at the poplars bending in the wind, left her stunned for a moment.

'Madame Delorme, would you like me to help you to the dining room?'

'Just coming, mademoiselle.'

She knows what to expect: she is to sit down at the place allotted to her, with paintings of countryside scenes on the walls, a landscape at twilight, a blue lake in the middle of a forest, a road with a church tower in the distance. This evening the menu is peaches stuffed with tuna, followed by chicken vol-au-vents, and some of the residents, the lucky ones, may even get a glass of wine. She takes the envelope out of her pocket and opens it. In the distance, she hears the noise of dinner being served. Her chair at table 5 will still be empty. She reads what

Marcel has said, and the rhythm of his breathing carries her away. The corridor leading to her room is full of pot plants and fire extinguishers, a safe refuge from any danger. Frédéric wanted something nice for her, and as it happens, his plan has worked. She won't be at table 5 this evening. No peach stuffed with tuna for her, no chicken vol-au-vent.

She finds the telephone book on a table close to reception. She has located his address in it: *Maisons-Laffitte*, and under the letter 'G', *Guedj*.

'Marcel, it's me . . . Come and get me!'

30

The rain beating down on the windows of the Peugeot reminds her of the enclosed space of a car wash. Marguerite tells the story of the last few days in a single long sentence. He asks no questions, and instinctively drives her to his apartment. He parks outside the unpretentious building and says, simply, 'You must have felt daring when you left that place.'

'That's exactly it. I finally dared to do something of my own accord.'

'I'm glad.'

'It isn't just about courage; it's a whole combination of circumstances.'

As she heads towards the boot of the car to fetch her bag, he stops her and takes her in his arms. Then he holds her steady as she goes up the stairs and leads her to his tiny sitting room, where he takes off her shoes, helps her to lie down, takes a blanket from the cupboard in the corridor and lays it gently over her fragile body. He sits down beside Marguerite, puts her legs on his knees and massages her feet. For a long time. And without a shadow of hesitation, she lets herself relax in this calm and reassuring atmosphere.

'All those white walls, all those lonely old people,' she sighs.

'I'm going to make us some tea,' he says quietly.

Marguerite watches the sky darkening over the town, spies some old cardboard boxes left out on the balcony, and a telescope.

'That little girl in Dunkirk . . .'

She falls asleep on the old sofa.

He puts the tray down on the coffee table and sits in the armchair to watch over her. He sees her face move as she has a bad dream, sees her white bandage, the blue of her bruised hand now turning yellow, her short hair all dishevelled, and he remembers wanting to take the hairpins out of her chignon that first day. He thinks of the eight-letter word 'intimacy'.

'My son's afraid I might meet the wrong kind of person.' That's what she had said on the terrace at Bagnères-de-Bigorre. She had blushed, and he had been charmed by that. What really touches him, goes straight to his heart, is the strange feeling that this woman had been waiting for him.

He doesn't know how long he watched her sleep in

his sitting room. He fell asleep himself. Only for a few hours. When he wakes at dawn, he doesn't feel at all tired; he gets up, opens the window and breathes in deeply. She is there, and it feels natural to him. He runs her a bath, switches on the heating. He stays nearby discreetly, leaving her to enjoy the warm water, the foam, the muted light from the lamp on the shelf. She comes into the bedroom, wrapped in a flannel dressing gown too large for her as if it were a familiar garment.

'Marcel, I borrowed the Maupassant from the library. You left out a bit. *Why these quiverings of the heart, this emotion of the soul, this languor of the body?* Would you like to close the curtains and lie down next to me?'

The phone rings in the hallway, and she says, looking mischievous, 'We're busy. Please do not disturb.'

He slips in beside her, murmuring, 'You're right – it's better to draw the curtains at our age.'

He undresses her in the dim light that smooths wrinkled skin. He perceives her fragile figure, her buttocks, her stomach, her neck. She closes her eyes and he brings his face close to hers and lays his lips on her velvety mouth. Just as he had in Collioure. Like tightrope-walkers treading delicately, they say in silence what they have not yet dared to express in words. Fear, desire, vertigo.

She touches his mouth with one finger, the bridge of his nose; she caresses the furrows of his face, the marks left by time, follows the course of a blue vein on the back of his large, wrinkled hand. Ravines and mountains, every mark, every line, she wants to know them all.

'You have the build of a very strong man.'

'In another life.'

She traces the fine white line that runs from his collarbone to his shoulder. 'What left that scar?'

'A tiger in a temper.'

He embraces her as if she were a delicate orchid, tracing curves round the angles, inventing caresses. Lace by lace, he undoes the invisible corset she has worn for so many years. He breathes her in.

'I love the scent of your skin.'

Marguerite's hands explore him, as if magnetised by the grainy texture of his worn skin, and he enjoys it. He trembles when she lightly touches the base of his back. Her hands are even gentler than he'd imagined. There are no disguises; this is the truth of their being. So old and yet so young.

He gently places his thumb on her eyebrow and slowly smooths it twice, first the left, then the right, and she smiles.

'Why are you smiling?'

'Because I feel good.'

'You're extraordinary.'

At this moment they are travelling without any baggage. They are free of prejudice, reason, other people's eyes.

'I like the smell of your skin too.'

Another embrace, a look, the fluttering of a wing. Their sleeping bodies are emerging from a long hibernation. Urgency directs their movements now; subterranean energies pulsate, easing their way out. Shameless, overwhelmed, they let themselves go, and pleasure lights up their faces.

The window opens; the curtain billows out; a ray of light falls on the floor. Spring comes into the bedroom.

With her head resting on Marcel's shoulder, she whispers, 'This is the first time.'

31

'I've been trying to find you for twenty-four hours. Where are you?'

'At home.'

'You're lying. This isn't your number.'

Sitting on Marcel's couch, Marguerite takes a deep breath and replies, 'I may be old, but not so old that I'll allow myself to be left in an old folks' home masquerading as a clinic without my consent. Nénette has been stuck there among the vol-au-vents and the stupid ventriloquists for ten years.'

'Who's Nénette?'

'It's no way to treat your mother!'

'I think we need to get you more thorough health checks.'

'What checks are you talking about?'

'Well, simply to check whether . . . whether your mind is still all right.'

'Being seventy-eight and going to bed with a man other than her late husband doesn't mean that a woman is demented.'

'Maman!'

'Whatever you think, Frédéric, I still have a life to live. Are you going to carry on telling me what I can and can't do all the time?'

She hangs up, murmuring, 'That'll do for now.'

She hears the front door open; it is Marcel coming in with his arms full of packages.

'I got some brioches and some oranges. What's the matter? You look a little odd.'

'I don't want to be at war with my son.'

He puts the breakfast shopping down on the table.

'Would you like a coffee?'

'I'd rather have a cup of tea, please.'

They both know they will have to face a lack of understanding. In their own ways, they have always avoided family quarrels. He sits down beside her and gently strokes her cheek. She looks at him and says, almost inaudibly, 'Life is so short. I could die tomorrow, and I don't want to be at odds with my son or anyone else.'

Frédéric puts down the phone.

'Well?' asks Carole.

'She hung up on me.'

'It has to be said that you've never listened to her. You don't want her to go out after six in the evening; everything has to stay just as it always was in that empty house. What's that all about? Pleasing your father?'

'I just don't recognise her any more. I didn't do it for myself; I wanted to protect her. We have to be realistic: she's an old woman, and she's wrong to think the contrary.'

'You're lucky that she's still around. Either you lose her earlier than you ought to or you adjust to the choices she's making.'

After two nights of questions to which he has no answers, he decides to phone his mother again. If he is honest with himself, Dr Dubois has never raised the spectre of even the slightest degree of dementia or early senility. He may have been wrong in envisaging the worst.

'Maman, forgive me for being so blunt . . . Life hasn't accustomed us to the unexpected. I wasn't brought up like that. Papa always had everything so well mapped out.'

'It's not a bad idea to be spontaneous now and then – you should try it sometime. Why don't you and Carole and Ludovic have dinner with us next Tuesday?'

'At your house?'

'No, at Marcel's apartment.'

. . .

Marcel and Marguerite have decided to prepare for the event together. She carefully chooses young carrots, leeks and peas in the market. Marcel is getting the veal, and insists on a very tender cut. He doesn't want to do things by halves.

She buys herself some violet-flavoured macaroons and enjoys them one by one with a delicious sense of freedom. He smiles, watching her from the other side of the covered market.

She joins him in front of the fruit stall; he takes her packages from her and kisses her with relish amid the cherries and the rhubarb, as if they had been separated for three days. In the queue waiting to be served, two ladies with their shopping bags in one hand and their dogs' leads in the other interrupt their chatter.

'Isn't that Maggy Delorme, the notary's wife?'

'She's cut her hair!'

'Less than a year since she was widowed and she's already parading her private life in broad daylight!'

'He's much younger than her. It's shocking!'

'A cougar in Maisons-Laffitte!'

The two dogs sniff each other's rear while the ladies at the other end of the leads carry on providing material for their local soap opera.

This year, the man at the fruit stall tells them, the Alpine strawberries are going to be delicious. Marguerite promises that they'll be back in early July, and is surprised yet again to find how much pleasure she feels at this very ordinary prospect. They almost forgot about dessert. Marcel suggests a cheesecake. Neither of them has ever made one, but they decide, with a smile, to embark on this new venture. Ludovic will love it, and the novelty will surprise Carole. For years Marguerite has been giving her a gâteau Saint-Honoré, bought from the best cake shop in town.

Marcel's kitchen is upside down. It's like action stations at a top restaurant: they are busy; they taste; they reread the recipe for the fifth time. The carrots could be sliced a little thinner; they will use the best salt, fleur de sel.

Marcel is in command, with a tea towel tucked into his waistband. On the menu, his own recipe for blanquette of veal, using cloves, plenty of cream, a glass of dry white wine and some sorrel at the last moment. He will keep a portion aside and take it round to his neighbour who lost her husband a few months ago; he feels he hasn't been thinking of her enough. Marguerite thinks of Nénette; they could pick her up from Beaulieu House one day, and all three of them could sit on the bench at Vincennes looking at the impassive figure of Hector.

Marcel shows her how to cut the leeks into little batons, and she puts her mind to learning, like a sous-chef. Simply for the pleasure of being with him, watching him stir the sauce in the casserole with his wooden spoon, or adding a pinch of nutmeg, trying to get the perfect balance of flavours. She reads the cheesecake recipe out loud, wondering whether it might be better to go and buy some raspberry ice cream. The simmering veal dish is giving off a delicious herby aroma that fills the whole apartment. Marguerite is gradually getting used to the cramped space here, and is comforted by the sight of her parents' silver-plated lamp, a painting that her sister had given her for her birthday, and beside their bed her little bedside table with *Madame Bovary* on it. She doesn't open the wardrobe containing the raffia handbag; she sometimes feels a pang of jealousy, but she knows some doors are better left closed.

Today she asks herself fewer questions about this man with his rough exterior and tender heart who moves about at night with a torch so as not to wake her, sleeps with his socks on, sings Chaâbi music on the balcony, and whose best friend lives in a zoo. A man who warns her that he will sulk if she listens to too much Line Renaud, but only for five minutes because he doesn't like sulking. A man who calls her his turtle dove, his swallow, his goldfinch. She relishes all that.

He asks her to taste the sauce with her eyes closed; she thinks there is too much pepper in it.

'You always have to add a few spices to a recipe or it'll be like life, too boring.'

And he punctuates this remark with a kiss.

She has bought a new tablecloth for the occasion, and she walks round the table laying the places, trying to work out where to stand to judge the general effect. She wants it all to be a great success. There won't be any local bigwigs as guests, and no Maria to polish the silver, only ordinary things that remind her of her modest origins and her childhood. Without proprieties or protocol, their family meals had always been convivial.

Manou arrives first, with a bottle of burgundy in her hand. A tall brunette in an attractive low-necked dress and a wise little lady – a Sempé character in the eyes of children – inspect one another. They are not really surprised. Some encounters are bound to happen, and they are both relieved.

'Wow, that smells really good.'

Manou takes the lid off the veal and dips her finger in the casserole to taste her father's sauce. He covers the casserole again at once, as he did when she was little.

'Papa is back at his stove – that's good to see.'

The bell rings three times. Two intimidated teenagers introducing their families to each other for the first time stand rooted to the spot in the middle of the hectic kitchen.

'It will be all right,' says Manou.

32

Opening the door, Marcel comes face to face with a huge bunch of red roses. This is his first sight of Frédéric.

'We'll never find a vase large enough.'

Frédéric shakes hands with Marcel and looks around him; he must be wondering why his mother left a four-star retirement home at Beaulieu House for this chicken coop.

Carole hasn't seen Marguerite since the retirement-home incident. To avoid this delicate situation, she busies herself with the roses, looking for a container that will take their tall stems. She fails to find one and eventually leaves them in the washbasin in the bathroom.

Ludovic flings himself into Marcel's arms. 'Papa wanted to get the biggest bunch of all.'

'And how's the champion driver?'

Proud as Punch to be dining with his teacher, he runs from the table to the telescope. Marcel takes the time to show him the Pole Star, telling him when it rises and sets. He promises that one cloudless night he will take him to see the star Margarita.

'Thank you for being good to my son,' Carole murmurs. 'He has no grandfather now, and I'm really touched by your kindness.'

Frédéric notices the watercolour that used to hang above the mantelpiece in his parents' house, now on the wall of this dining room. Manou raises her glass to the engaged couple, looking straight into the eyes of Maître Delorme, who is biting his lower lip. In a clear and joyful voice, she says, 'I keep thinking of all those evenings when I didn't dare phone my father because I was afraid I'd find him absolutely crushed by grief. Life certainly does keep some nice surprises up its sleeve.'

Marcel puts his hand on Marguerite's.

They talk about the rain that has been deluging the country for the last three days, and Ludovic's progress at tennis. They congratulate Marcel on his blanquette of veal. And Carole says, to the company at large, 'That's the best cheesecake I've ever tasted.'

Marcel drinks some wine, clears his throat and announces that he would like to take Marguerite to sleep in the trees in the Cévennes. 'In the heart of nature, a wooden tree house five metres above the ground.'

Frédéric jumps. 'What about her knees? That's insane!

If she gets up there, she might never be able to come down.'

'She has wings now,' Marcel ventures to say. He knows that reality will catch up with his wild desires, and he presses his leg against Marguerite's under the table. One day you might climb a tree not knowing it was for the last time.

Carole looks at them affectionately, then turns to her husband. 'How about you, Frédéric? Would you ever take me to sleep in a tree house? Would you roll up your shirtsleeves and haul up the basket with the bottle of red and the Camembert inside?'

'Let me point out that I didn't wear a tie this evening and you didn't notice,' sighs Frédéric. 'It's the same with my stubble . . . I'm trying to look more up to date, but all you see is my starchy side.'

'Last week you gave me a present for no particular reason, and when I undid it, I found a bonbonnière – something no one has used in the last thirty years! Talk about being up to date . . . Really, there are times when I don't understand you.'

Everyone laughs to lighten the atmosphere. And then the talk turns to Meryl Streep's latest film, marriage for all and the one-way traffic system in Maisons-Laffitte, which is about to be reversed in some of the local streets. Ludovic has fallen asleep on the sofa. Without effusive promises to meet again soon, the evening comes to an end. Carole wakes her son gently and says he can come back to the apartment soon.

Frédéric tells Marcel quietly, 'All of this is new to me. My father died last year, and it's not so easy to hand my mother over to someone I barely know.'

He clumsily kisses Marguerite on the cheek. She forgets to thank him for the flowers, and peace returns to the apartment.

Marcel is proud of the little speech that Manou gave with such simplicity and such kindness. She really is Nora's daughter. This has been no ordinary family get-together. He particularly liked pressing his leg against Marguerite's; a good thing the tablecloth wasn't too short. It made him lose the thread of the conversation, dreaming of the moment when they would be alone and he could take her in his arms.

'There, that's over and done with,' she says.

'It was your idea, and a good one.'

'I'm happy.'

'You look tired.'

When he put his hand on hers during dinner, she held her breath and then returned his caress.

'I'm not used to being in love.'

33

Curled up under a soft eiderdown beside Marcel, Marguerite can't get to sleep. She feels as if she is on a high wire, about to fall, and the orange light of the street lamp that sends shadows dancing across the ceiling light adds to her fears.

He loves giving her surprises and has found a charming inn, exactly the kind she likes. It rained heavily this afternoon, the large sitting-room window has a pretty view of the drenched garden, and there was something about this place, overflowing with books and photos, that made them feel like staying in beside the fire. Marguerite, surprised to find that she wasn't missing the sun, basked by the hearth on the sofa.

The woman who owns the inn collects teapots. They are all over the place, lined up on the furniture and the shelves. China teapots, metal teapots, teapots with ornate spouts. She told them the story of some of her teapots with almost carnal delight, her voice full of enthusiasm.

'I'm a merry widow. These teapots saved me.'

And Marguerite, looking at Marcel, thought, We all have our own lifeline.

If she had met him when she was twenty, would they have made waffles every Sunday to the sound of their children's squeals and laughter? Would the whole family have plastered what was left of the waffle mixture over their faces? She might have lived in an old house in the country with three goats and five sheep, and she would have called out, 'Marcel, when you've finished feeding the chickens, come and taste this dessert. I think I've invented a new recipe. Maybe we can make some money with it!'

In the little bedroom in the middle of the night, she plays the leading role in this imaginary existence. Infants running about in the meadows, antiseptic ointment for grazed knees, guests coming and going, sitting at the large wooden table; she is the matriarch presiding over this happy pastoral scene.

Where did she go wrong?

She thinks she spots two large catfish above the wardrobe, but they are only decorative jugs transformed by the nocturnal shadows.

She knows that in spite of the successful dinner she

organised at Marcel's apartment, she will be able to count family dinners on the fingers of one hand, and she trembles before this love story and the radical change it has made in her life, so late in coming. She loves his caresses, and she fears her own addiction to that sweet – that very sweet drug. The previous evening he had left a poem under her pillow:

> We often speak or want to hear
> Of that great lord or beggar dear
> We talk of that wild poet who
> First invented rendezvous.
>
> We speak of him with no aim
> Just for the pleasure of his name
> For his mystery and his flame
> Made from laughter, and from pain.
>
> We speak his name, so sweet to hear,
> Even when we may shed a tear
> We murmur it low in the night
> When his strange powers do us unite.
>
> We speak of it when it is new
> And when we have lost it too
> We laugh at it from time to time
> Yet seek it out, the search sublime.

We celebrate it, loud and clear,
Until one day it shows so dear
That Love, that wanderer of great fame,
*Takes on a single person's name.**

She is overwhelmed by the man. How can she measure up to everything he is offering her? Where can she find a user's manual for love, when she isn't even capable of climbing on a chair to change a light bulb? Men mature, women grow old, or is it the other way around? Should she obey her instincts? If only someone could tell her.

At five in the morning she has a brainwave. Several wives of prominent citizens in Maisons-Laffitte have taken that bold step, in spite of their husbands' disapproval, and now she has decided to take it herself. One more silly decision won't make a difference, but she tells herself that no one will ever know. Not even Marcel. Her sudden decision sets her mind at rest, and she falls asleep at last, lulled by the orange light of the street lamp falling on the catfish above the wardrobe.

One week later she hasn't changed her mind. Saying that she has some shopping to do, she sets off towards the racecourse. Walking down the road, which is dark even though it is a sunny morning, she remembers that her

* Jacqueline Dalimier, 'Des ailes au bout des doigts'.

sister went for a similar consultation one day. When she came back, she didn't want to tell her anything about it. All that Marguerite had been able to gather was that her sister had found the visit disturbing. All the same, she likes revisiting some of the episodes of Hélène's life, because it is almost like seeing her again, like a momentary mirage.

On the door of the small apartment, a notice says, *Bell out of order*, and when the lady who lives there opens the door, Marguerite can't find anything to say. Old photos on the walls depict racehorses in training. There is nothing to suggest that she has come to the right place.

Madame Delvaux is Belgian by origin, and in the local area people say that, twenty-five years ago, she had predicted the death of King Baudouin in the summer of 1993. Her prediction was correct.

With a pleasant smile, the clairvoyant asks her to shuffle the cards carefully, then spread them out face down, pass her hand above them several times and concentrate as she chooses four. No crystal ball or black cat, which is reassuring. She turns over the first card.

The names of the symbols on them echo in her head, but she is lulled by this tall, dark woman's melodious voice. She ought to have come here sooner.

Madame Delvaux says that she is facing new opportunities, and Marguerite trembles, disturbed to find that the cards already know that much about her. She hears the clairvoyant say, 'The Sun, and a better world . . . The Moon, evoking the subconscious mind, hidden forces and the possibility of disappointment.' She shivers when the next card proves to be the Serpent: she sees herself going straight to hell. Before they began the séance, the clairvoyant gave her a cup of tea, but Marguerite is unable to drink any of it. She is gripped by fear, as if she were about to learn that her life stopped here, in this building, in front of some black-and-white photos of racehorses.

There is still one card to be turned over. Madame Delvaux tells her that if the last card drawn is the Star – the symbol of peace, protection and good luck – everything should turn out well, since it corrects the negatives.

'Stop!'

Marguerite pays what she owes, and in an attempt to shake off her uneasiness, she adds that the horse photos are very pretty, just as a person would talk about anything and everything with their doctor to delay the moment of hearing the diagnosis.

A few moments later she is out on the pavement, clutching her handbag close to her coat. She walks more slowly than she would like; aches and pains are never far away when you are growing old. She ought to have confined herself to asking about her wretched knees; that would have been a more sensible option. She doesn't want to know the future. She knows she must simply hope for the best, and if the worst happens, life may still have some surprises in store. That old woman in Beaulieu House knew what it was all about: life in spite of the rubble.

On her way back to Marcel's apartment, she stops at the grocer's to buy flour and eggs. This afternoon she will make Belgian waffles.

34

Two disobedient urchins, that's what we've become. We refuse to listen when we're told to be careful, we'll catch cold, that's not sensible, stay in and watch TV instead. We don't want to be sensible, and we feel that we know the jingle introducing *Countdown* by heart. Sitting still for so long makes our bottoms ache. We need suitcases, travel guides; we need to discover new horizons, as far as the eye can see; we need yet another change of scene; we need to warm our old bones in the sun, breathe in different scents, to go into the church in a little village that we don't know. To enjoy every last bit of life while we still have the strength to do it and legs strong enough for us to go off the beaten track. We're always talking, like two mutes who have recovered the power of speech. We have a galloping desire to take advantage of every second, even if we have to sleep for a week to recover when we get back.

'What if I were to take you to see some wide open spaces, my turtle dove?'

'Can't my globetrotter ever stay put?'

'I want to see new landscapes.'

'Let's leave on Monday.'

Wild horses and bulls in gypsy country, a log cabin straight out of a picture book, a single-storey cabin with shutters opening to reveal the Lac des Mystères, citronella candles to keep the mosquitoes at bay. That would be the Camargue.

'We won't stop off anywhere else on the way, and once we're there, we'll walk round the lake and watch the colours changing with the light. Then we'll count the pink flamingoes.'

We count fifteen on the first evening. Free, majestic birds, they fly off into the dusk. We are careful in our different ways: a thick roll-neck sweater, like something a truck driver would wear; a dress that is too light for the time of year – one of us overdoing things, the other too restrained. We won't change our ways, and this time it won't take us fifty years to realise it; that's the advantage of late-blooming love.

The next day, with our trouser legs rolled up, we paddle in the lake, holding on to each other so as not to slip in the mud.

'It's a lot nicer than those mudbaths.'

'And there's no alarm going off.'

'And no toads wearing flip-flops.'

The water is cold, and we shriek when something slimy brushes against our calves.

'Do you think that was a piranha?'

'Only some pondweed, sweetheart.'

'I've waited seventy-eight years to take off my ankle socks and paddle in a lake with a man.'

We sit on a rock, our movements slow. Even putting a pair of socks back on after taking them off is laborious these days and gives us trouble. We smile because it's such a nuisance.

'Some things are so much more difficult that we'll have to live one day at a time.'

'Together?'

'Oh, do be quiet, you idiot, and do up your shoelaces.'

At Saintes-Maries-de-la-Mer, in the crypt below the altar of the church, there are thousands of lighted candles, photos and letters from the gypsies who have come to ask for the blessing of the Black Virgin. We shall never come back to this place, and that certainty makes the hours we spend there magical.

'I don't know what I've done to deserve such happiness, Marcel. I won't go down on my knees because I'm afraid I might not be able to get up again. Otherwise I'd ask you if you'd like to spend the rest of your days with me.'

'And who knows, I might even say "yes", my swallow, I would.'

The return journey isn't so easy. As if life sometimes wants to make us regret being so bold. It doesn't take much to disturb the harmony. A defective cylinder head gasket, in this instance. We have to stop on the hard shoulder, taking refuge on the little slope above it like two shipwrecked sailors while we wait for the breakdown truck to come and find us.

'I think I'll set out on foot.'

'You're never going to march away across the countryside with your wonky knees and this torrential rain!'

'I've always heard that there are only limited chances of survival on the hard shoulder of a motorway.'

So there we are, two old people wearing fluorescent yellow jackets, getting cross with each other and waving our arms about. The arrival of help curtails any idea of walking.

There's no appealing against the verdict of the man in charge, who is small, sturdy, bald. If we want to get home, we'll have to go by train. We reassure one another as we cope with the fear that our hearts are tired after all these adventures. The breakdown man helps us to climb the step up to the cab of his truck. Between a calendar showing naked Barbie dolls and a photo of two small children clinging to their mother's neck, our unlikely trio heads towards Avignon Station. The bald little man tells us about the misfortunes of other motorists, and the patience he sometimes needs to deal with their whims and fancies.

'There was even one guy who wanted to sleep in my truck. There are weirdos all over the place!'

We're amused by this unusual situation; we'll have a funny story to tell Ludovic.

When we get to Avignon, we hesitate to call our children and ask them to come and rescue us, and end up deciding not to, in case they put up a fight the next time we want to go away on our own.

The station hotel looks inviting, and hoping to nibble a few more crumbs of happiness, we whisper ideas to each other.

'We could give ourselves an extra night's holiday.'

'Only if they have a double bed.'

35

Marcel has brought her a cup of tea in bed, as he has done for the last ten years, before they have breakfast together in the kitchen. He has woken her with a kiss, has put a second pillow behind her back to make her more comfortable and has got back into bed beside her to do his breathing exercises.

'I'd like to go to Paris,' murmurs Marguerite.

'Aren't you happy here?'

'What if we went there today? It's been such a long time.'

'You're right. It feels like the other side of the world, but it's only eighteen kilometres away.'

'I'd like to see the Place des Vosges again, and the Grands Boulevards.'

'It's something of an expedition, but for you, my turtle dove, I'm ready for anything.'

'At our age, we can allow ourselves a few follies from time to time.'

'The Peugeot's not very reliable these days, and the stairs on the Métro are too steep. I'll get us a taxi for the day; it can take us anywhere you want to go, and then we can play at being Japanese tourists.'

Marguerite has chosen to wear a summer dress, a flowery jacket and a lilac shawl that she found at the back of the wardrobe. She smiles in the bathroom mirror as she meets Marcel's eyes; his eyebrows are now as white as his thick hair. He kneels down and delicately does up her shoes for her. She thinks he looks elegant in a linen suit that he hasn't worn for ages. He takes his walking stick, and the two old lovers carefully go down the stairs, after turning off the gas and checking twice that the door is locked.

On the leather seat of the taxi, she says the first place she would like to visit is the block of apartments where her sister lived: on the Quai de Valmy with a view of the Canal Saint-Martin. That will be the first stop. She automatically reads the names on the letterboxes: Lebrun, Renard, Benzaken, Bartolini. Names, like lives, are forgotten, but the grey stone of the building is still there, intact. A woman with her back bent is placing several pots of geraniums on the ground-floor windowsills.

'Can I help you?'

'I've come to see where my sister used to live. Her name was Hélène Jacquet.'

The caretaker slowly straightens up. Hélène Jacquet. The name sounds vaguely familiar, but she can't remember why.

'Thank you, madame. Goodbye. I very much like the colour of your geraniums.'

Memories can be cruel, although sometimes you deceive yourself into believing in illusions. Marcel wants to go back to the station where he arrived with his parents in 1954. Their taxi drops them at the passengers' entrance. The wooden benches have all gone now, the building has changed a great deal, and he tries to familiarise himself with the station with tears in his eyes. Marguerite affectionately strokes his cheek. How can anyone stand up to these dizzying journeys back to the past?

On leaving the station, they walk at random in Paris, that insolent and eternally young metropolis, keeping step with its boisterous rhythm. She marvels again and again at the beauty of the city in the June sunlight.

By common consent, they decide to go and see Victor Hugo's house under the arcades of the Place des Vosges. They support one another and lean on one another, cling and nestle together. In the noisy, fast-moving capital, Marcel and Marguerite celebrate the pleasure of moving slowly. Victor Hugo seems to exist outside time, and briefly he reassures them.

Marcel suggests a cappuccino in a bistro in the Rue des Francs-Bourgeois, doing violence to their delicate digestion, he says. As she sits down by the window, Marguerite feels the familiar tension in her coccyx. Sometimes aches and pains get the upper hand.

'I haven't met anyone nice in Maisons-Laffitte since Dr Dubois died.'

'Don't worry, we'll see about that tomorrow. For now Paris is opening its arms to us.'

They will finish the day with a riverboat trip on the Seine. It's by no means their first time on the water: Marcel had looked at the map of France, drawn circles round all the navigable waterways, and they had promised themselves that they would travel down one of them each year. The first time they went from Rennes to Nantes. They had been lucky, as the Bretons say: the weather had been fine several times a day. Marcel saw himself as a riverboat captain, and Marguerite waved to the people walking along the towpaths. She was attending art classes, watercolours, and had embarked on a series of sketches of the little houses beside the locks. In the evenings she proudly showed them to him, and he told her, smiling, that she certainly wasn't cut out to be an artist. One day, much later, he had to admit that their boat trip down the Canal du Midi would be the last one.

Between the Pont de l'Alma and the Pont Neuf, she whispers that she owes Dr Dubois a large candle.

'I told you before we got our cappuccinos that we'd do that tomorrow. Look at the sky above Paris, my dove – it's travelling along the water with us.'

'But I do owe him a candle,' Marguerite insists. 'He sent me to Bagnères-de-Bigorre, and if it wasn't for him, we wouldn't be here now. I enjoy everything I do with you. Before meeting you, I was living in the slow lane. I like the person I've turned into when I'm with you. Thank you for a lovely day.'

In her handbag, she has the card that she stole from the clairvoyant years ago while the latter was looking for change. She sometimes looks at it without understanding its meaning. An old man in a heavy woollen robe is holding a stick in one hand and a storm lantern in the other. The red lettering says, *The Hermit*.

Marcel kisses her lovingly, and the clouds in the sky above them carry on their wild race.

'You're the surprise that I wasn't expecting. I've never had any luck gambling, but that day on the terrace I won first prize. And that's leaving aside Ludo. I mustn't forget to get the envelope ready for him this evening.'

Tomorrow they have two things to celebrate: Ludovic has passed his baccalaureate, and he is going to introduce his new girlfriend to them. She works at L'Heure Bleue, the new tearoom in Maisons-Laffitte.

On the landing stage, Marguerite squeezes Marcel's hand very tightly in hers; she wants to ask him a favour.

'Did I ever tell you that my sister used to live on the Quai de Valmy? I'd like to go back and see that apartment building someday.'

36

'Ludo has told me so much about you, and it's a pleasure to meet you properly for the first time,' says Apolline, smiling. Then she goes on serving her customers.

Ludovic's eyes are shining, and Marguerite remembers the conversation they had years earlier. He did finally climb the rope ladder, he has lost his puppy fat, and now he is a tall, slender young man with curly hair. What kind of lover will he be? Will he be ardent like Hélène or stuffy like Henri? Will he be more extrovert than his father, or will he have inherited his mother's tenderness?

Do you need weapons or just luck to be successful in love? Anyway, he has laughing brown eyes, and that's a decent asset to begin with.

Marcel looks at the beauty of youth without bitterness, in the way one looks at everything that is ephemeral.

. . .

Apolline brings them three glasses of lemonade and some lemon meringue tartlets, and then moves away, flitting from table to table, light of foot, like a silvery dragonfly. Ludovic, in a talkative mood, tells them about the exams, especially his dissertation on philosophy, his favourite subject. The theme was, 'The force of circumstances, destiny or chance?' His grandmother has been talking to him about that for years, and he got the best marks in his class.

Marcel takes an envelope from his pocket.

'This is from both of us. Driving lessons, as a souvenir of the first silly thing we did together. When you've passed the test, you can drive us around this town.'

'I'll take you anywhere you like.'

Eighteen, that's when you have to start making choices. Marguerite has known for a long time that he won't be either a notary or a gymnast. But he won't be deciding yet, not today in this tearoom.

'You could travel,' she says.

'A year's voluntary work abroad,' Marcel suggests.

'I don't know – there are so many possibilities.'

'You'll find the right way for yourself,' says Marcel. 'Take your time.'

'I love getting postcards,' adds his grandmother.

As she drinks her lemonade, she enjoys this moment of happiness given to her by her grandson. She looks at the jeans that are too large for him, the floppy hair that keeps falling over his forehead. What a gift this boy is! She is delighted by his close relationship with Marcel. She will support his decisions, whatever they are.

They say goodbye to Apolline before leaving the tearoom. Ludovic kisses her as you might enjoy the first mouthful of a warm roll just out of the oven. Marguerite smiles as she looks at Marcel, and they decide to walk round the park and smell the freshly cut grass.

Marcel's cane with its intricately worked knob gives him the look of a gentleman born, which does not displease her. One shop window leads to another, so slowly that Ludovic has to make an effort to adjust his speed to theirs, his frail grandmother leaning on his arm. He concentrates on finding the right rhythm. She goes gently, because these days she has to.

He leads them to the bench facing the château; she shivers, and Marcel puts his cashmere scarf round her neck to protect her from the breeze.

'Don't move. I'm going to take a photograph. You look so good sitting there, both of you.'

Jutting cheekbones, hollow cheeks, deep lines, weary bodies. They are fragile, in the twilight of old age. But no shadow of loneliness rests upon them.

Leaning back on the bench, Marcel looks at the tree-tops, telling himself that he never did take Marguerite to sleep in a tree house. She is as tranquil as a lake on a windless day. Her face, her attitude reflect the peaceful certainty of knowing that she is loved. His large hands, the texture of parchment, stroke her small, wrinkled ones.

They do not talk, yet they are telling each other so many things. Eighty-three and eighty-eight years old, but those years do not add up. Time is suspended for as long as the taking of a photo lasts, and Marcel and Marguerite are young and immortal.

As he fixes that moment in time, Ludovic is aware that it will accompany him for the rest of his life. Someday the photo will be in a frame, and a guest will ask, one evening, 'Who are those two old people sitting on a bench?' and he will reply, 'My grandparents. They were a remarkable couple.'

He smiles and adjusts the focus of his camera.

'The light is splendid. The green of the leaves behind you and the colour of your coat, Granny – it's perfect.'

'Will you give us an enlargement?'

This may be the last time anyone takes a photo of them, thinks Ludovic. He takes another.

A little boy has just put his toy boat on the water. It sails briskly along. The breeze ruffles Marcel's hair.

Marguerite leans towards him and murmurs, 'We should go to Paris someday. It's been so long since our last visit.'

Marcel draws his white eyebrows together. He glances at Ludovic, holds Marguerite firmly in his arms and replies, in a steady voice, 'I'm here.'

blog and newsletter

For literary discussion, author insight,
book news, exclusive content,
recipes and giveaways, visit the
Weidenfeld & Nicolson blog and
sign up for the newsletter at:

www.wnblog.co.uk

For breaking news, reviews and exclusive competitions
Follow us 🐦 @wnbooks
Find us 📘 facebook.com/WeidenfeldandNicolson